IN A WINK

IN A WINK

•

Lacey Green

AVALON BOOKS
NEW YORK

© Copyright 1999 by Kim McDougall
Library of Congress Catalog Card Number: 99-94439
ISBN 0-8034-9362-2
Published by Thomas Bouregy & Co., Inc.
401 Lafayette Street, New York, NY 10003

PRINTED IN THE UNITED STATES OF AMERICA
ON ACID-FREE PAPER
BY HADDON CRAFTSMEN, BLOOMSBURG, PENNSYLVANIA

For Larry: Captain, my Captain

Chapter One

Kara Mackenzie closed her appointment book and rubbed the tension from her forehead. She was a beautiful woman, in an unassuming way, but the strain of the past months showed on her face. Her normally generous mouth was pinched in a frown, her long auburn hair was untidy, and her green eyes were circled with shadows as if she had not slept in many nights. Kara knew she looked haggard, but the farthest thing from her thoughts was concern for her own well-being.

She gazed out of her office window at the sun setting over the Montreal skyline. With a sigh, she put her agenda aside and turned to a stack of files that had been awaiting her attention all day. Her staff had already gone home, and the outer offices of In-A-Wink were quiet.

Well, why not? she thought. *Only the boss needs to work late on a Friday night.* Annie, her tireless assistant, shuffled in, arms laden with packages of Chinese food.

1

"Even the boss should get a Friday night off once in a while," she said. Annie had an uncanny ability to read Kara's thoughts. Had it been anybody else, Kara would have found the intrusion distressing, but Annie had been with her since In-A-Wink was just a fledgling business, and Kara still sold her photographic accessories out of the back of her car. Annie knew the industry as well as Kara, and she knew Kara even better.

She knew, for instance, that for the past six months, since the breakup with her fiancé, Kara had worked too hard and slept too little. She also knew, though Kara had not yet spoken of it, that In-A-Wink was in serious financial trouble.

"What would I do with a Friday night off?" muttered Kara, her nose deep in a file of submission requests. Last year she would have left this paperwork to someone else, but a lot had changed in a year, and Kara now insisted on seeing every slip of paper that passed through the office. She didn't trust her staff anymore, a lack of confidence that stemmed from a deep and painful mistrust in herself.

Annie gently pulled the file away and replaced it with a paper plate. Kara sighed. There was no point in resisting Annie's ministrations, and the smell of sweet and sour chicken had made her stomach respond with a gurgle.

"Well," said Annie, as she doled out heaping portions from each container, "if we had a Friday off, we might try those new roller skates over at the rink. My grandson says they're awesome."

"They're called blades, Annie. Roller blades." Kara grinned, imagining the pair of them on roller blades—Kara with her gangly, uncoordinated legs and Annie with her too straight back and prim skirts.

"A fine pair we would be, eh?" Annie winked at Kara. "A couple of *ta-ta's* on wheels."

Kara laughed at the French expression. Annie's accent made her sound like a sexy starlet from the nineteen forties.

Kara knew that Annie was only diverting her attention away from the day's worries, but she let it work. It felt good to stretch her imagination, to think of something else besides numbers, budgets and contracts.

They ate in silence for a few moments. Kara had not eaten since breakfast. She suspected that, in the excitement surrounding this afternoon's announcement, Annie had forgone lunch as well.

In-A-Wink had been accepted as the exclusive Canadian distributor of a line of German-made lenses. It was a major coup for In-A-Wink, one that could propel the company into a leading position in the Canadian market.

Kara let her mind wander over the day's events. She had been at the office since dawn, preparing to meet with the directors of Prolar, the lens manufacturers. Her day had alternated between positive hype and flattery on her part and mild threats on theirs. Finally the deal had been made, signed, and was in a plum sauce–stained file on her desk. This deal had the potential to thrust In-A-Wink far and beyond her competitors. It could also, much more easily, plunge them into the frightening abyss of bankruptcy. It had been a calculated risk, one that Kara had no desire to second-guess now. She changed her line of thinking.

"You know," she said, "if I had asked any other woman"—*especially my mother,* she thought—"how I should spend my Friday night they all would have suggested that I find a date."

"Mmm," said Annie with her mouth full, "especially your mother."

"Yes," said Kara, "especially my mother. But you didn't mention that and I'm grateful."

"Grateful, nothing. When you're ready to date, you will. Just as when you're ready to talk about Matthew, you will." Kara started to protest, but Annie was unconcerned with her objections.

Kara's silence about her broken engagement troubled Annie. She didn't want all the gory details—after all, the whole industry knew the gory details. Rumor had it that somebody was circulating the office security video of their final confrontation.

No, Annie didn't want to hear the details. She just wanted Kara to talk about it, to know that she was finally able to put it aside. Annie scooped up the empty containers and paper plates and left Kara's office, quietly closing the door behind her.

Kara often thought about Matthew, about being with another man, of putting herself in the position to be humiliated again. It made her palms sweat. Not that she feared placing her trust in someone else. It was more that she feared trusting her own judgment of character. She had been so horribly wrong the last time.

Kara would not be surprised if Matthew himself was circulating the tape. He had already shown that he had no sense of shame. Six months ago he had left In-A-Wink, taking half of the company's clients to the competition. It was a trap that she had laid for herself. She should never have become involved with her top salesman. Always careful to acquit herself with grace, Kara had finally stumbled into the web of the old boys' network that was the photographic industry.

It wasn't as if she hadn't anticipated this; she had. In fact, she and Matthew had discussed it, and they both had agreed that no matter what, business was to be kept separate. She had made two colossal mistakes, however. First, she didn't get it in writing. Second, she had overestimated Matthew's honor as well as his feelings for her.

These misjudgments, more than Matthew's betrayal, irked her. You didn't become number one in this tough business by being careless, and In-A-Wink had been the number one distributor of photographic accessories in Canada before Matthew's defection.

She had made a fatal mistake, and now her company, her baby that she had nurtured for so many years, was paying for it. Never had she believed Matthew capable of such betrayal—not toward her but toward In-A-Wink. For the past two years she had thought of it as his company as much as her own. She had imagined them running it together, building an empire to pass onto their children. Matthew had had other ideas. His vindictive reaction to their breakup showed a side of him that she had not even guessed at.

Darn you, Matthew, she thought. *And you too, Kara.* Not for the first time she wished for someone to take the responsibility of scolding her, as if she had brought home a poor report card. *But I'm the boss now. Nobody scolds the boss.*

She put some files, specifications on the new line of lenses as well as details of the contract, in her briefcase to look over in bed that night. The lenses would have to be repackaged and marketed for the Canadian trade. Hopefully other exclusive lines would follow before the big Photokina consumer show next fall in Germany. She had cash now, but if she didn't invest it wisely, there would be layoffs by next year.

She sighed. When work became no fun, as it often was these days, it was time to go home. Even Annie, who was usually the first to arrive and last to leave, was gone. Only the cleaning lady remained. As she left, Kara smiled and waved to her over the noise of the vacuum.

The Chinese food had settled like a lump in her stomach and Kara felt queasy on the ride down to the lobby. The paisley design of the elevator's wallpaper blurred in her tired eyes and the bright lighting made her head throb. Thoughts of her bed started to seem very inviting. Maybe she would put aside the stack of files just for one night. She deserved it. When the elevator doors opened, she lurched out and slipped on a piece of cloth that lay on the floor. Ragdoll-like, her legs flew up into the air and her arms flailed uselessly. She landed on her bottom with an ungraceful *thump*, knocking over an empty paint can in the process. Her skirt flew up to expose her legs to the thigh.

"*Mon dieu! Madame, s'cusez moi!*" The man looked down on Kara, her long bare legs splayed at a painful angle, auburn hair tousled in her face, papers strewn all around.

"It's all right." She let him help her up and then smoothed down her skirt. "I'm fine."

"You are," he said with a grin.

He said it in a way that sounded like a come-on. Kara looked up at him angrily, only to meet the most startling eyes she had ever seen, gray-blue, like the absence of light at sunset, and with long curling eyelashes; they twinkled as if he were laughing.

"That was some fall," he said. His accent was fainter now, but she realized that it was only his French lilt that had made his words sound like a come-on. It was the same accent that made dowdy old Annie sound like a starlet.

Suddenly the tensions of the day eased from her and she laughed with him.

"Yes, I suppose it was. If clumsiness was an Olympic event I'd be on the podium."

He smiled and stooped to pick up the papers that had flown out of her briefcase. Kara watched him and was struck by how, in contrast to her own clumsiness, he seemed so nimble. Within seconds, he had her papers arranged and was busy cleaning up the bit of paint that she had spilled.

His loose painting clothes accentuated his broad shoulders and long legs. He had dark curly hair that was also flecked with paint, though Kara suspected some of the white to be natural. She guessed him to be in his late thirties, but his boyish smile made him seem years younger.

"You're an artist," she said, realizing how mundane the comment was, but he was smiling at her with his stunning blue eyes and she could think of nothing else.

A hundred women must have told him that he has beautiful eyes, she thought, feeling giddy.

"Actually," he said, pointing at the mural, "today I am a writer." For the first time she noticed the mural that he had been working on. It was a poem. Words written so tiny as to form the lines of a drawing. From only a few steps away the words were invisible and they became two faces—one dark, one light—blended together as one.

The effect was so astounding that Kara couldn't help uttering another inanity.

"You did that?"

Kara didn't have an artistic bone in her body. She couldn't write, sing, or draw. She could barely even dance without precipitating disaster. Feats of creativity always impressed her, but this mural was truly something special. She started to read it, following the lines around the heads, but it was written half in French and half in English. The two languages ran together to form long incomprehensible sentences.

"What does it say?" she asked.

"Oh, your standard inspiration about working together in harmony. The owners of the building wanted something motivational. I told them to go buy posters of whales, but they insisted on something unusual. I hope they meant it. Do you see here, where their hands meet?"

Kara nodded. He grabbed her sleeve and pulled her over to the right.

"That's cooperation. And here, where the lips turn up in a grin?"

She nodded again. His enthusiasm was contagious.

"That's wit. And here, risk."

He pointed out details that Kara had not even noticed, explaining how each added to the picture as well as complemented the others. He was clearly passionate about his work, and Kara was a bit envious. It had been many months since she felt the same about her own job. His fingers dug into her arm possessively, as if he was afraid she would leave. Kara knew, at that moment, nothing could drag her away from this strangely dynamic man. He chattered with schoolboy enthusiasm, though his voice was deep and smooth. Kara found herself equally fascinated with the painter and the painting.

When he had exhausted his artwork's possibilities, though clearly not his inspiration, the artist turned his startling eyes on her and asked, "So what do you think?"

Kara was out of her depth.

"I . . . I think it's beautiful," she said honestly. "I just feel kind of sad that most people will miss those subtleties."

"You think so?" He cocked his head to one side and stared at his work with a critical eye. "You may be right." He frowned, exposing long dimples on either side of his mouth. Kara had to resist the urge to reach out and trace them with her finger.

"Then again," he continued, "you may be giving your fellow man a raw deal."

"Perhaps," said Kara. "Poetry has never been my forte."

"Mine neither. I just do it to pay the bills."

The way he said it, so matter-of-factly, was reassuring. He might have a mind gifted beyond Kara's imagining, he might seem possessed by a muse when he spoke of his work, but even he had to pay the bills. That was something Kara could relate to. She smiled and held out her hand in a businesslike manner.

"My name is Kara."

"Michel," he said, making the name sound like a caress. "*Enchanté, mademoiselle.*" He took the tips of her fingers in his paint-stained hand and bowed deeply over them. She thought she felt his lips brush her skin, but the sensation was so gentle and so fleeting it might only have been his breath.

"An honest critic is above all value," he said, but

Kara wasn't certain if he was teasing her or not. Maybe her remark about subtlety had been unsubtle. She felt herself flush with embarrassment and was about to apologize, but Michel was already absorbed in his work again. With his paintbrush gripped in his teeth, he studied the darker face and carefully smudged the area around the eye with his finger.

"Well, I'll be anxious to see it finished," said Kara. He smiled at her, still clenching the paintbrush. The muses had reclaimed him.

Kara felt awkward watching what now seemed like a private moment between art and artist. She headed for the main door of the lobby, wondering at her own self-consciousness. She was usually a confident, self-possessed woman. In the span of a few minutes Michel, the painter, had managed to anger, excite, and then embarrass her. Was it some power the handsome artist could command over her, or was there a greater problem? She had spent the past six months, since Matthew's defection, second-guessing her motives for everything from salary increases to lunch orders. Maybe her shyness with Michel was only the beginning. Maybe she had finally managed to undermine her own self-confidence.

Kara looked back at Michel, who was busy adding touches of paint to the background. She watched his shoulders flex as he stretched to reach the top of the mural. She realized that it was something much more basic that had made her act so foolishly. He was an incredibly attractive man. But so was Matthew. Suddenly reclaiming her self, she had an idea.

"Have you ever done any product design?" she called back to him. Michel straightened, turned to her, and removed the paintbrush from his mouth.

"I studied in graphic art," he said, clearly curious.

"When will you be finished with the mural?"

"Monday morning."

"Come up to my office, top floor." Her words were crisp and sure. She was back in her element. "I have an interesting proposal for you."

Michel shrugged.

"I'll be there."

Outside, Kara walked to her car with a curious sense of elation. The air was cool, but she was warmed by an inspiration of her own. Michel was just the person to design their new lens line. He was flamboyant and yet classy. She stopped herself: His *work* was flamboyant and classy. Whatever. In her gut it felt right, and she was so glad to have that intuition back. Her impulsive hunches had made In-A-Wink a success. Only when she had let go of her impulsive nature, when Matthew had tried to tame it out of her, had things gone awry. For the first time she had real hope for the coming season.

Chapter Two

"Annie, I've been looking at these estimates for caterers." Kara chewed on the end of her pen as she had since high school. A sudden image of the painter with the paintbrush clasped in his lips flashed through her mind, and she pushed it away. She had been watching the clock all morning, wondering if he would show up. Their meeting from the night before replayed continually in her head so that it took considerable effort on her part to concentrate on paperwork.

"I just think that we can't afford the staff party this year."

"But it's tradition," said Annie. She deposited a stack of checks to be signed on Kara's desk. "Wine must be spilled and food must be devoured to pay proper homage to the gods of industry."

"That's the worst excuse for a party I've ever heard," said Kara with a grimace. She thrust the stack of estimates at her assistant. "Seriously, can we afford this?"

"We can't. I agree," said Annie. "Let's start a new tradition: the company barbecue. I'll speak to the girls in the secretarial pool. Everybody can bring something. I hear that Dave in accounting makes the best chili this side of Texas, or so Dave says anyway."

"Chili?" Kara wrinkled her nose in distaste. "Have we sunk so low?"

Annie ignored her sarcasm.

"All you have to do is supply the barbecue and the pool."

"I don't know . . ." Kara let the words drift off. She stared at the view outside her window, but Annie knew that Kara wasn't seeing the beautiful Montreal skyline. Her thoughts were somewhere else, somewhere they had been far too often lately.

"Money is not the only reason that you want to cancel this party, is it?" Annie glared at her with one eyebrow raised.

How does she do that? thought Kara. *Always inside my head. And that eyebrow! My mother can't give an evil eye so well.*

"Perhaps," continued Annie, as smoothly as if she were suggesting a cup of coffee, "you're wondering if everyone will remember last year's party?"

Last year Matthew had asked Kara to marry him with the whole office staff as his witness. She would not have said no anyway, but she had been irked that his public display had not given her that option. Everyone had *oohed* and *ahed* when he produced the ring. She could have done nothing else but accept it

gracefully. A warning bell had clamored in her head
that night, though. How could Matthew, the man she
had chosen to spend the rest of her life with, know
so little about her? Surely he should have known
how much more she would have cherished the moment had he proposed in private. It was only the first
time Matthew showed her a side of him that she
didn't particularly like. His controlling manner made
him an excellent salesman, but it eventually became
the chisel that drove them apart.

"I guess you're right," sighed Kara. "It's still so
vivid in my mind. I can't imagine that anyone else
has forgotten it." *Or what came after,* she thought
to herself.

"No, they haven't forgotten," Annie said bluntly,
"but now, more than ever, the staff needs a boost of
morale. Besides, you can't punish them for your
mistakes."

"Ouch, Annie. That hurts."

"Not as much as living with a disgruntled staff
would."

"Again, you're right, but let's at least push it back
until the end of June so that when I push you in the
pool you won't get pneumonia."

"You're the boss," said Annie with a grin. She
turned to leave. "Oh, by the way, there's a Michel
Vernier waiting to see you. He's got paint all over
his clothes. Should I let him in anyway?"

Kara had finally managed to forget about him. The
mention of his name so startled her that she couldn't
even manage a witty rejoinder. She simply nodded.

"Sorry I am such a mess," said Michel standing in the doorway to her office. "I just finished the mural downstairs." His pants and shirt were stained with paint as the night before.

"That's okay," said Kara, "we're very informal around here."

"I see that. They made me wait ten minutes in the reception." He said it sternly, but his grin gave away his carefree attitude. Even from across the room Kara could smell his perfume: oil paint and turpentine mixed with something else, heady like musk.

"Chloe, the receptionist, was probably just hogging you for herself," laughed Kara. In her own territory, away from his intimidating mural, Kara felt more in control of herself so that she could even flirt pleasantly without those horrible feelings of inadequacy that she had experienced the night before.

"But everything worthwhile is worth waiting for, don't you agree?"

He nodded. Kara led him by the arm to the meeting table at one end of her office. In-A-Wink took up the top floor of a downtown building, and Kara's office had a spectacular view. Not wanting to detach from this natural wonder, she had decorated sparsely but with elegance. Seemingly without effort she had mixed marble tables with natural woods. Her desk was a rich mahogany, as was the large meeting table. The couch was a deep green leather. The end tables and bookshelves were natural granite. In these familiar surroundings, the awkward woman who had tripped over a paint can the night before was just a faint memory. She smiled at Michel and offered him coffee.

When they were seated comfortably, she indicated the line of lenses that were laid out with their boxes on the table. The packaging was a respectable blue with black lettering. Kara knew that if she left them like that they would take their place on store shelves beside other dreary boxes and wait for the whim of a salesclerk to be shown. She needed something exciting—something that would make the consumer demand to see her lenses, something that the retailer would be proud to show off in his window display. All this she intended to convey to Michel, but not yet. First, she wanted to see his reaction. She wanted to know if his instincts matched her own.

As he took a moment to examine the samples, Kara studied him. His was a startlingly handsome man with dark curling hair and finely drawn lips rounded by a short fuzzy beard. And yet, had she passed him in the street, with his rumpled, paint-stained clothes and three-day beard, she would not have given him a second glance, not because he was not handsome but just because he was so poorly dressed, though Kara suspected that his painting garb was only a costume that he wore. He carried himself with a sureness, an elegance, that was as inspiring as his mural. He seemed to wear his rumpled clothes with pride, as if sticking his nose up at conventions. That he was singularly out of place at the elegant meeting table only enhanced his appeal. In the close proximity of the office she was drawn to him. That

self-consciousness crept in again, and she was glad
to begin the meeting. As long as she spoke of cameras she could keep the fluttering in her stomach to
a minimum.

"Nice lenses," said Michel.

"I'm glad you think so, because I want you to
package them."

He didn't protest, but he didn't agree right away
either. Instead, he sat for several minutes inspecting
a lens. He fondled it, feeling the texture of the ex-
terior casing. He turned the zoom ring and listened
to the mechanism shift inside. Kara was impressed
with his thoroughness.

"You seem to know about cameras," she said.

"A bit, but only as they relate to painting. I often
photograph my subjects as reference."

Finally he put the lens down and turned his big
eyes on Kara.

"Graphic art is not my strong point anymore," he
said. Still, it was not a protest, but a simple statement
of fact. "Why do you want me?"

Kara realized that she had been holding her breath.
She let it out quietly, not wanting to show him how
crucial this really was.

"I don't want to go the usual route with these
lenses. I don't want just a blue box with black lettering. I need something that's going to move. Something exciting and classy."

Something to save this company from utter ruin,
she thought to herself.

"I take it you have no idea what that something
is?"

"That's your job," she answered smartly.

"I'll need your help."

"You'll have whatever you need."

"Fine," he said, getting up. "Meet me at the old port tomorrow at two."

"Does that mean you'll do it?"

His eyes twinkled with a sense of humor not altogether appropriate for the setting.

"For you, mademoiselle," he said, flourishing an imaginary hat, "I would steal Apollo's fiery chariot and race it across the heavens." With that peculiar farewell he was gone.

Kara sat for a long moment alone at the meeting table.

"Inspiring, I suppose," she muttered, getting up. "Strange, but inspiring."

She went to her desk and opened the file on the top of one pile. She stared at it, but she didn't take in anything that she read.

She hoped that she was doing the right thing. In-A-Wink did not have the money to waste on a marketing failure. But somehow, in her gut, Kara knew this was going to work. An even tinier part of her dared to hope that it would be a huge success.

For the rest of the afternoon the office smelled faintly of turpentine. Kara, working diligently through the folders on her desk, tried to ignore it.

May had been the coldest Kara could remember, with temperatures often dipping low enough for snow flurries. In the beginning of June, however, as Kara waited at Montreal's old port, the sun shone like midsummer. She was glad that she had taken the time to go home and change into jeans and a light cotton blouse. She wore her hair back in a ponytail and on her feet she had her old cowboy boots. She didn't know what Michel had in mind, so she had dressed for comfort.

She strained her eyes to see up and down the boardwalk. The port stretched along the St. Lawrence River for a good half-mile. As it was already after two o'clock, Kara worried that she was not waiting in the right place. In front of her was St. Jacques Square, lined with outdoor cafes. The winding cobblestoned streets had been turned into a pedestrian walk, and dozens of local artists and artisans peddled their wares from portable kiosks. It had the flavor of a medieval market and was the central tourist attraction of the old port. Kara had assumed that Michel would meet her here.

''You look worried,'' he said, coming up behind her.

''You're late,'' she snapped. Kara hated tardiness in herself as well as in others. It was one of the few neuroses she had inherited from her mother.

''No, I have been sitting over there for almost half an hour.'' He pointed to a bench half hidden in the garden square. ''Look.'' He handed her a sketch pad. The port was realistically depicted in pencil: the gardens, the cafes, the artists, and in the background a large ship unloading its cargo. Leaning against a rail was a girl with worry furling her brow. She had a long ponytail and wore jeans and cowboy boots.

Kara gazed at the picture of herself. It was not how she remembered her image from the mirror that morning. Gone were the tired circles under her eyes. Gone were the slouched shoulders. The drawing was more alive than she felt—beautiful, really.

Is that how people see me? she thought. *Or just how he sees me?* Aloud she said, "You're forgiven."

"Good. Now let us have something to drink before getting started. I need you relaxed. Did anyone ever tell you that you are strung as tight as a bow?"

"You think I'm tense?" laughed Kara. "You should meet my mother."

"I would like that," he said, pulling her along by the elbow.

He picked a cafe that had a terrace overlooking the busy pedestrian walk. Their table was made for romantic encounters. It was just wide enough to hold their two glasses and a pitcher of iced tea. They were secluded, but their view was not entirely obstructed, by the flower boxes that hung over the terrace railing.

This was the first time that Kara had seen him in real clothes. He wore jeans and a denim shirt. They were worn but neatly pressed. His shirt was unbuttoned to show a bright white undershirt with a tuft of hair peeking out above the collar. He smelled more of musk than of turpentine. Kara was suddenly aware of how close they were and how romantic the little cafe was—definitely not her usual business setting. Michel seemed relaxed, as if he knew the sights of old Montreal well and could let them pass by while he sipped his iced tea.

"Look at that couple sitting across the way," he said, indicating the terrace on the other side of the square. "They are breaking up."

Kara glanced at the couple. The woman leaned forward and spoke quickly, gesturing now and then with her hand. The man looked down at his drink and nodded dejectedly.

"Not by his choice either, it seems."

"You are observant," said Michel. They watched the couple for a few minutes. "I wish I had a camera with one of your lenses right now. That is a very poignant picture."

Kara was encouraged. Their instincts did match.

"That's exactly why I hired you," said Kara. "Somehow, I'd like to capture that poignancy in the lens package. Cameras capture the beauty of this world, and I think it's shameful that the boxes they come in are so traditionally ugly."

"And that is why I brought you here. We're going to spend the afternoon observing people and hopefully the cool drink will calm you, as it already seems to have done," he said with a smile, "so that I get a better idea of what you are after. Have another glass." As he filled her glass, Kara watched his hands. They were long-fingered and moved with a deft control. She had a fleeting image of them on her skin, on her arms, perhaps, pulling her toward him. He spoke to her, and though—or maybe because—

she concentrated on the deep curve of his lips, she did not hear his words. He had shaved his stubbly beard, and his smooth skin seemed only to accentuate his mouth. Without the beard his lips became the most prominent feature on his face. How could she have not noticed them before. It was his eyes, she decided. They were such a startling shade of blue and so darkly lashed that one tended to ignore the rest of his face. She was certain that many women had fallen in love with those eyes. She wondered if any one ever noticed his mouth. Maybe she was the only one.

Suddenly she realized that he had asked her a question and was waiting for a response. He grinned at her, but she refused to be embarrassed by him yet again. She was, after all, a successful businesswoman who had extricated herself from many an embarrassing situation before she ever met Michel Vernier. It was time she put him in his place. He had laughed at her enough times. She would finally show him her mettle. In-A-Wink was not built by a frivolous girl, after all.

Perhaps she could upset his calm confidence with offensive maneuvers.

''I was just wondering if anyone had ever told you that you have a beautiful mouth.'' She said it with a sort of authority that precluded flirtation. She fully expected him to at least feign embarrassment. Instead, he furrowed his brow, as if thinking back to all his past compliments.

"No," he said, "I don't believe that anyone ever has."

Kara wanted to kick herself under the table. To cover up her own embarrassment, she said quickly, "So what was your question again?"

"I asked if you had considered your marketing strategy beyond shaking things up."

"Of course I have," she snapped, and then added, "but what do you mean?"

"Well, who are you going to target?" Michel didn't look at her but continued to scan the crowds. "Any Joe Blow off the streets?"

Kara tried to keep her voice even. He seemed to imply that she didn't know her business. She may not have seemed like a professional in her jeans and cowboy boots—her remark about his appearance didn't help, she knew—but darn it, she had been in this business all her adult life, long enough to know her target. Once again, she realized with a sinking heart, she was dealing with a man who assumed that just because she was young and pretty and female, that she didn't have a brain in her head. He probably thought that Daddy built the business.

Well, she thought, *I may know nothing about art, but never let it be said that I don't know my way around the camera industry.*

"No, it's not an impulse item," she said, sounding strangely formal. "This is usually a well-researched purchase."

"Professionals?"

"No." She sipped her drink. She was starting to

enjoy this. "A pro would buy the brand name that went with his camera. But anybody else with a reflex camera. The real question is, who buys reflex cameras?"

"It's a luxury item, then," he said. Kara shook her head.

"Not really, but look at that family and assume the mother is a single mother." She pointed to a mother with three small children licking ice cream cones in the square. "Would they have a reflex camera?"

"Well, compact cameras tend to be more practical," said Michel tentatively. Kara felt the thrill of ego. Michel now understood that she knew her business, and he was choosing his words carefully. "And less expensive. But if they were avid camera buffs . . ."

"A single mother tends not to have the luxury of being avid about anything but her kids," said Kara.

Michel looked around. Kara was right; the young mother was alone.

"These are hard facts of life," she said, "but I have to make some choices about who I want to target. Now look over there." She pointed to a thirty-ish couple leaning over the port rail. The man had a reflex camera slung prominently around his neck.

"Your instinct about wanting excitement is right," he said. "Those are the people who will buy your lenses, and they already think their lives are very exciting. They'll buy the gadgets to suit them."

Kara had been chauvinistic in her own way, she

realized. She had assumed that Michel, an artist, would have not one iota of business sense. She was pleased to be proven wrong.

"What about him," he asked, pointing at an old professor-type who was taking pictures of the ship in dock.

"Oh, forget him. He has been taking pictures since before Mr. Eastman," said Kara, referring to the founder of the Kodak company. "He has got his camera and his lenses and will not be changing for anything new in this lifetime."

Michel sipped his drink and smiled at her. He, too, seemed pleased that they were on the same wavelength.

"So the yuppies it is," he said.

"And the students," she added. "They don't have much money, but that might work to our advantage. The line is not too expensive."

"Good. Now that we have that settled"—he reached across the table and covered her eyes with his warm hand—"close your eyes." She did. "Now, when I say open them, tell me what is the first color you see." He took her head in both his hands and gently turned her neck so that she faced the garden in the middle of the square. "Now remember, don't think about it, just say the first color that you see. Open your eyes."

"Yellow," she said immediately. "I see the yellow tulips."

"Exactly. The boxes should be yellow."

"But yellow is so gaudy," she said. "I was thinking of something more classy, like hunter green."

"Green is a background color," he said. "If we were painting your living room, I would agree, but we are not. We are selling lenses. And yellow is not always gaudy."

"We haven't talked about prices," she said. He looked at her quizzically. "Your fees, I mean."

Michel shrugged.

"I'm not a businessman. We will talk prices after you see my first mockups. For now, I just have to say . . ." He paused and stared at her with a half-smile. "I just have to say that I am really enjoying this, and that you have a tiny piece of lemon rind stuck to your cheek."

Kara blushed and wiped her mouth with her napkin.

"You missed," he said. "May I?"

She nodded. He leaned across the tiny table and gently wiped the lemon away. His hand lingered on her face, stroking her chin with his thumb.

"Did anyone ever tell you that you have a beautiful mouth?" he asked wryly.

Mesmerized by his blue-gray eyes, Kara just shook her head.

When his mouth met hers, it was the softest kiss, like the wind that blew through the terrace. After what seemed like many minutes, he let his hand drop and sat back.

"I guess I shouldn't have done that," he said, looking almost sheepish.

"What?" She felt dazed. She reached up to touch her lips that were still tingling with the kiss.

"Kiss the boss-lady. I hear it is not proper."

Kara froze with her hand halfway to her face. She wanted to forget about propriety, about responsibility and success. She wanted to forget about In-A-Wink and how much she needed this man to bring the company back from the brink of bankruptcy.

But the word boss-lady galled her.

The last time she had an relationship with an employee, it had almost cost her the business. Michel would be on contract and not exactly an employee, but could In-A-Wink stand another one of her glaring lapses in judgment?

Suddenly her only thought was to get away from this dangerously attractive man, to put enough space between herself and temptation that she could begin thinking with a clear head again.

"Excuse me," she said, pushing back her chair, "I have to go to the ladies' room." For a moment everything was blurred. Vaguely, she sensed her toe catch on the leg of Michel's chair, and she fell with a crash.

The waiter was instantly beside her, but Michel pushed him away and helped her up. She had landed on her knee on the cement terrace, ripping her jeans. Her skin underneath was also torn and bleeding.

"*Mon dieu*, Kara," said Michel, staunching the flow with a napkin. Her face was ashen, and he tried to keep his tone light. "I knew you were clumsy, but I didn't know that you were into self-mutilation as well.''

''I haven't pierced my navel yet, if that's what you mean,'' she said, trying to sound brave. The sight of her own blood made her queasy. She closed her eyes. From what seemed a great distance, she heard Michel ask the waiter to fetch a clean cloth. When he returned, Michel wrapped the cloth tightly around her knee to staunch the bleeding, and then he picked her up and stood her on her feet.

''Can you walk?''

''I think so,'' she nodded. She felt him kiss the top of her head gently before putting his arm under her shoulder. Through her wooziness, Kara thought it was the strangest kiss, like the way one kisses a child. She let herself lean on him, using the throbbing pain in her knee as an excuse not to pull away. Together they hobbled out of the cafe.

They took her car home, though Michel insisted on driving. Kara didn't protest. She disliked driving at the best of times. It took her several minutes to unlock her front door. Her fingers were ice-cold and stiff, and they fumbled with her hefty ring of keys. Michel did not take the keys from her, but simply stood behind her, supporting her weight. Kara knew that his closeness had much to do with her clumsiness.

Michel led her upstairs to her bathroom where he poured peroxide on the cut. Once it was cleaned, it didn't look nearly so bad, and she let him administer to it without complaint, even when he told her that she would have to take her jeans off.

"I won't look," he said with a grin. "I promise." He left the bathroom and came back with a pair of cotton shorts.

"I didn't even go through your lingerie to find them," he said. Kara didn't react to his humor. The heat had drained her, and her knee had started to throb. Besides the cut, tomorrow she would have an awful bruise, but these hurts were nothing compared to the one that was inside her—the one that had just begun to scar over, only to be torn open again by Michel's kiss.

"Are you okay?" he asked, brushing her disheveled hair from her face.

"I'm fine." She pulled away from his touch.

"Hey, I'm not going to kiss you again. There are sharp objects about," he said. "Who knows what you will do to yourself." She didn't even smile.

"Come on, I'm kidding."

"I know. I'm just tired."

"Here, take these. That leg must be throbbing." He handed her two aspirins and a glass of water, and then he helped her off the counter.

Downstairs he saw her comfortable on the couch and tucked a blanket around her. He made sure that she had the TV remote and then left her to go fix sandwiches.

"Really, Michel," she said when he came back. "You don't have to do all this. You make me feel like an invalid."

"I am paying homage," he said, handing her a plate. "I've never seen anyone take a tumble like that."

"Oh, it's nothing," she said, regaining some of her sense of humor. "I do it all the time." They ate their sandwiches and watched the news, and then Michel said that he would catch a cab back to town. Kara didn't protest.

After he had left, she sat on the couch for several hours, watching but not paying attention to the various sitcoms that played. Even her throbbing knee was little diversion. Something with a potential for disaster had happened to her that afternoon, but no matter how long she denied it, it would not go away. It was in her stomach fluttering like a butterfly; it was in her lips, tingling like a static shock; it was in her hands, itching to touch his face.

She could not stop thinking about the kiss, not the one on the lips, but when he had kissed the top of her head. It had been so spontaneous and so affectionate that it had set alarm bells ringing in her heart. She knew that she wanted to see him again and not in the board room. How easy would it be to fall in love with Michel and forget her commitment to In-A-Wink?

What if his work was horrible? Would she be able to put her feelings aside and tell him the truth? She thought of firing him right away and hoping that he would understand her position, but like all good curses, hers was double-edged. What if firing him was the wrong thing to do for In-A-Wink? What if firing him brought on the disaster she hoped to avoid? She agonized over these questions all evening until, finally, she fell asleep with the television shining in her face.

She woke before dawn feeling stiff and bruised. Though she knew that everyone would remark on it, she wore a bandage wrapped tightly around her knee as a reminder of her own foolishness. She had more than three weeks before Michel was to present his first mockups, twenty-five days to agonize over her decision.

Chapter Three

June 24th, St. Jean Baptist day, the biggest summer holiday in the city and the first annual In-A-Wink barbecue, dawned bright and warm. Kara laid out a sundress and a bikini for the afternoon. She was not yet sure if she would brave the bikini, though she knew most of the girls would.

Annie was the office mother and confidant to the employees. Even before the Matthew fiasco, Kara had been known to keep her distance from her staff. She had always told herself that she needed to keep her objectivity, but in truth she had always been a loner. She had worked hard, mostly by herself, for many years, and now that the company had expanded to include over a dozen employees, she discovered that it was not so easy to be a team player. She let Annie be her link to the others, even more so since Matthew's betrayal. It was better that way. Nonetheless, when she walked by the lunchroom and the conversation stopped, she felt a pang of loneliness. She could never be one of the girls.

She put away the bikini. Her leg was still scarred anyway. In the three weeks since her outing at the old port, her knee had healed, though the skin was still a tender pink. She poked at it tentatively as she pulled on her shorts. She had not seen Michel during these weeks, though she had spoken to him on the phone. He was to present his mockups on Monday, two days away. She found herself looking forward to the encounter with mixed feelings. She had turned down his invitation to lunch last week. She wasn't sure if she could trust herself to share even a simple meal with that man. Even the memories of standing close to him were intoxicating. Until he was finished with the packaging for the lenses, until she had no more need to speak to him as an employer, she must keep her impartiality, and that meant keeping her distance.

As she pulled on a cotton T-shirt, the phone rang with the distinctive double ring that signified a long-distance call.

Kara cringed inwardly. It was most likely her mother.

Monica lived to the south of the island of Montreal, a half-hour's drive past the bridge. Fortunately for Kara, the distance was just enough for Monica— who was always preoccupied with her finances—not to call too often.

What could she want today? Kara wondered. *Hopefully not an invitation to the party.* Kara understood her mother's shifting moods enough to know that Monica need not want anything in order to aggravate her only child. Kara picked up the portable phone and continued dressing.

"Hello?"

"Hello, daughter. Remember your old mother?"

Kara could tell by Monica's trembly voice that she was on the upswing of a depression. Her mother's mood swings had been traumatizing to Kara as a child, but when she grew to understand such things, she began to suspect that her mother suffered from a chemical imbalance resulting in depressive behavior. She had never been able to convince Monica to seek professional help, but just knowing that her mother could not keep back her hurtful words helped Kara deal with it.

She was glad to hear Monica's attempt at good humor, though she'd been fooled by her cheerful words before. Kara didn't want to deal with her mother's troubles today.

"Of course I haven't forgotten you, Mother," said Kara, unconsciously adopting a soothing voice. "We spoke only a few days ago."

"Yes, and I seem to recall that I made the long-distance call that time, too. Really, Kara, you could be more considerate. You act as if I have money to spare."

"You're right, Mother. I'll be sure to phone next time."

When Kara's father passed away, he left enough money for Monica to live more than comfortably, but Monica preferred to remember this only when it suited her purpose—like when planning Kara's wedding. For the most part she acted as if she still had to live frugally, as in the early years of their marriage when they had lived in a tiny, barely furnished apartment on Montreal's poorer east side.

But Kara didn't want to argue with Monica today. She finished dressing and began to tidy her bedroom, only half listening to her mother ramble, until Monica hit on the one topic that Kara could not ignore.

"I saw Matthew yesterday," said Monica in a tone that tried to sound ordinary, as if she spoke to Kara's ex-fiancés every day.

"What do you mean, you saw him?" A sense of foreboding crept into Kara's voice. Matthew also lived on the south shore, but it seemed more than a coincidence that he should bump into her mother.

"He dropped by for tea. Nice man, really. Never could understand why you broke off with him."

"Tea?" asked Kara. Matthew disliked tea almost as much as he disliked her mother.

What could he possibly be up to? Her train of thought was cut off by Monica's next pronouncement.

"I told him that he should drop by your place today to say hello to his old co-workers."

"You did what? Mother! How could you be so foolish? Do you think anyone from the office wants to see him?"

"Kara, really. You shouldn't let your own feelings make you selfish. I'm sure the others miss Matthew terribly. He was very well liked, you know."

"Did he tell you that?" asked Kara sarcastically.

"Well, yes, but it's rather obvious. He's a charming man. And he misses you terribly, Kara. He talked about nothing but In-A-Wink."

Suddenly Kara understood Matthew's thinking, and the realization filled her with as much anger as it did dread. Matthew was using her naive mother as a corporate spy. It would have been ridiculous if it wasn't so desperate, and unfortunately Kara had seen Matthew at his most desperate. It wasn't a pretty sight.

"You know, Mom," Kara tried to keep her voice light, "if you keep entertaining the enemy, then I won't be able to tell you all the office gossip anymore. He might find some way to use it against me."

"Kara!" Monica sounded indignant. "Do you think I would leak your secrets?"

"Not purposely," said Kara. She knew that her mother couldn't keep a secret to save the world, but she never told Monica company secrets. Monica was just not interested in business. She still spoke about In-A-Wink as if it were an amusing hobby that Kara would eventually outgrow.

"But Matthew is a salesman, Mom, and he needs to prove himself to his new employer."

"You sound so paranoid," laughed Monica. Kara held the phone away from her ear and made a face.

This from the queen of paranoia, she thought.

Her threat seemed to have the desired effect, however. Monica loved gossip, especially about her daughter's life.

"All right, dear," she said. "I'll tell the big bad

man not to come by anymore. But just tell your poor mother one more secret before hanging up. Is there anyone else yet?''

''Um . . . no.'' Why did she hesitate? And why did those startling blue eyes appear in her mind as if by conjuring. Luckily Monica did not notice the awkwardness in her response.

''Well, keep Mother up to date, and you call me next, understand?''

''Yes, I will.''

Kara sank down on her bed, ignoring the clothes laid out there.

Why did she have to call today?

The conversation had drained her. Speaking to Monica was always a challenge. She had been no better or worse than Kara had come to expect. What really troubled her was the casual reference to Matthew. What was he playing at? Did he really expect to insinuate himself in her mother's life in hopes of getting at Kara, or worse, at In-A-Wink? All her life—perhaps from watching her own mother's deterioration—Kara had fought paranoia and the extreme emotions, but her gut told her that she was not wrong. Matthew was up to something. The sheer audacity of visiting Monica worried her. For the two years of their relationship, Matthew had not been shy about voicing his opinion of Kara's mother. Monica was sick, he had said, and should be committed. When Kara refused to concede this, Matthew cut off all contact with her family; Kara went to weddings and holiday dinners alone.

And now Matthew had stopped by for a spot of tea with Kara's demented mother. That Monica still admired Matthew was proof of his charm. He was up to something, though. He had an obvious vendetta against Kara and In-A-Wink, and she wondered how far he would take it. *Maybe this party wasn't such a good idea after all,* thought Kara. She didn't feel much like playing hostess. Thank goodness Annie would be there to take care of the details.

She arrived at noon to prepare the tables and the food. Kara had spent the morning rewiring the stereo so that the speakers played out on the deck. She vacuumed the pool and the house and then helped Annie lay out platters of hors d'oeuvres. That morning's conversation with her mother replayed in her head over and over again.

"Forget about it," Annie said, steering her toward the bathroom. "Tonight is for fun, not for thoughts of unstable mothers. Go soak in the tub for half an hour. Everything is just about done."

Kara gave in without much fight. Despite the heat, a warm bath sounded soothing. She added extra bubbles and sank gleefully into their depths. Bubble baths relaxed her, the steam sweating her skin, the tiny curls clinging damply to her temples. Her thoughts turned to Michel. She was becoming dependent on her memories of him. They were like a reward for good behavior—if only she could get through this stack of paperwork, if only she could dial Monica's number, drag herself out of bed and then through the day—if she could do all these things, then, when she was alone, in the bath or tucked under her duvet, she could grant herself a few thoughts of him. In the swirling, scented heat of the bathroom, only one image appeared in her head—Michel hovering over her as if he were bending to kiss her. She did not see his face, but recognized him by the curve of his neck, the rich, tanned skin that led up to his earlobe and a few curling hairs.

"Time to get out, before you to turn into a prune," hollered Annie from the other side of the bathroom door. Kara sighed. Her reveries were burst as much as the bath bubbles that had dissolved in the water.

"I'm coming." She grabbed the chain with her toe and pulled the plug, letting the water and bubbles drain away, enjoying the shock of cold air on her wet skin.

Instead of feeling more relaxed, Kara was strangely energized. For the first time, she found herself looking forward to the party. She decided to take Annie's suggestion and, for one night, to forget all the stresses in her life. She would forget about her anxious mother, about Matthew, and the coming buying season. If she was lucky, she might even be able to forget about the painter, but even as this thought entered her head, she knew that was unlikely. Every man she met, old or young, handsome or not, intelligent or not, was compared to Michel.

Well not tonight, she thought. *Tonight I am as carefree as a young girl.*

She dressed in her deep red sundress, leaving her

hair long and loose. It had not yet gained its summer highlights, but still, it was a rich brown and she knew it to be her best asset. She put on little makeup except for a dark red lipstick to match the dress. She slipped on sandals and, as an afterthought, a gold ankle bracelet given to her by an ex-boyfriend.

When she came downstairs, Annie had transformed the house into a fairyland. Streamers and balloons decorated the living room and patio. Baskets of flowers adorned the picnic tables, and candles in tall bamboo holders were stuck in the ground around the pool to be lighted at sundown.

''Annie, you're a marvel!''

Her old assistant just smiled. She didn't even look tired. Not for the first time, Kara wondered where she would be today without Annie. She was responsible, in no small part, for the success of In-A-Wink, and though she had not spoken to Kara about their current financial situation, Annie was shrewd enough to know that they faced severe downsizing in the spring.

It must break her heart as much as it does mine, thought Kara. *Maybe that's why I can't bring myself to speak of it.*

She was arranging hors d'oeuvres on a platter as she had these thoughts and realized that already she had broken her promise to herself.

Perhaps it's not possible to get away from one's life for an evening.

Annie watched Kara out of the corner of one eye as she prepared a heaping bowl of potato salad.

Kara's face was tensed with a concentration that the hors d'oeuvres didn't merit. Her brow was furrowed and her lips pressed together in a flat line.

Annie watched her for a few minutes and then said quietly, "Tonight is for fun, Kara."

Startled, Kara looked up from her platter.

"Right." She grinned sheepishly. "Tonight is for fun."

Annie frowned and gave Kara her best evil eye.

Tonight is for fun, Kara repeated to herself like a mantra. *Tonight is for fun.* But the good, sensible part of her—the part that signed the paychecks and slept alone in her king-size bed—knew that she had forgotten how to have fun.

Kara was adding the ice ring to the punch when the first cars pulled into the driveway. The girls headed immediately to the bathrooms to change into bathing suits while the men just shucked their shirts and dove into the pool in their shorts.

Every staff member showed up, except Chloe, the receptionist, and most had brought dates, so that within a very short time, the patio and pool were alive with excited voices. Claude, her controller, had fired up the barbecue, and already she could smell delicious things roasting. Kara circulated through the crowd offering drinks. She realized that she was dressed perhaps a bit too formally, as everyone else wore shorts or bikinis, but then she noticed the flirting glances that the girls in the pool received from the men, and decided that—fun or no fun—she was better off on the sidelines. She could play the part of the dignified boss-lady.

No reason the boss can't have a glass of punch though, she thought.

As she poured herself a glass, there was a commotion from the pool house behind her. Jason, one of her salesmen, had found the pool toys, and had equipped himself with every piece of water paraphernalia he could find: goggles, snorkel, flippers, floaties, shark fin, water gun, and, around his middle, a big yellow duckie inner tube.

He ran out of the pool house, hollering ''Take no prisoners!'' and spraying everyone with the Uzi-like water gun. With two long strides, he cleared the deck and cannonballed into the middle of the deep end. When he surfaced, the girls immediately dunked him and stole all his toys.

''And you said a barbecue wouldn't be a success,'' said Annie, coming up behind Kara to refill her punch glass.

''Yes,'' replied Kara, ''that was so exciting.'' She pointed at the front of her dress where a stain darkened the fabric. ''I spilled my punch when Jason shot me. I'd better go clean up.''

Since the dress was red anyway, she decided not to change out of it, but just to dab it with cold water. She went downstairs to the powder room that doubled as her laundry. As the party was mostly contained outside and in the kitchen, the basement was dark and quiet, except for the faint thump of music. In the laundry room, a dozen handkerchiefs were folded in a pile on the dryer. She grabbed the top one and then almost put it back. It was one of a set of monogrammed linen handkerchiefs that Matthew had given her for her last birthday. Kara thought they were a conceit, but Matthew had insisted that if women could wear business suits, they should wear hankies, too.

"Especially the boss, Kar," he had said, tucking the handkerchief perfectly into the pocket of her blazer. "You want people to take you seriously, don't you?"

He knew she did. As a young female executive, she had often struggled against the old boys' network that dominated the photography industry. However, she had never been able to understand how a hankie, puffed out of her lapel, made her more businesslike. Still, she shouldn't use it to sop up a stain. It was an expensive gift.

Oh, why not? she thought spitefully. *Tonight is for fun.*

She plunged it under cold water and pressed it to her ribs where the stain was the worst. She worked at it for a few minutes, struggling to reach around to her lower back.

"Would you like some help?" said a deeply accented voice. At first Kara didn't react. She had been listening to his voice in her head for so many days now, she thought it was her imagination, until, in the mirror, she saw him standing in the doorway behind her.

"Michel?" He was so out of place in her basement laundry.

He just grinned at her.

"You really are a clumsy woman, eh? Every time we meet you have an accident. Here, let me help you with that." He took the hankie from her and began dabbing at the stain. With him standing so close to her, Kara was grateful for the cool water on her skin. She was painfully aware of his hands rubbing her back, even through the layers of dress and handkerchief.

What was he doing in her house?

He was dressed in a golf shirt and shorts. His dark curls were tamed back except for one unruly lock at his temple. His stubbly beard was shaved clean. She thought that she must be having some kind of waking dream, a hallucination brought on by stress. Though it was some hallucination. She looked down at the water flowing from the tap. It was real, and so were the sink and the silly monogrammed hankies. And Michel's hands that continued to rub at the curve of her waist.

"What are you doing here?" she blurted. He seemed unconcerned by her confusion.

"The bathroom upstairs was being used." He washed out the hankie which was stained pink.

"No," she stammered. "I mean here, in my house?"

"Oh, I'm somebody's date."

Of course, thought Kara. *Why hadn't I thought of that?*

"Chloe found herself alone tonight and was kind enough to invite me."

I bet she was. Kara thought of her well-poised receptionist and knew the sting of envy. Chloe was always polished. She exuded a confidence in her own femininity that Kara could never feel. Kara could not imagine Chloe skinning her knee at a cafe or spilling something all over herself.

"I'll bet Chloe never fell over your paint can on her bottom." She tried to sound witty, but to her own ears her voice rang with jealousy.

"No, as a matter of fact she did not." Most of the time, Michel's accent was barely discernible, but now and then—Kara didn't know if it was due to anger or nerve—his sentences were stilted, without any contractions, as if he were searching for his words. To Kara he sounded exotic, like a nineteenth-century novel of manners.

"Ooh la la!" Michel whistled and pointed at the embroidered monogram on the hankie, KSM. "Fancy."

Kara wrinkled her nose.

"Yes, they are a bit pretentious. They were a gift."

"So what does it stand for, KSM?"

Kara could not stop the next words that tumbled out of her mouth. Later she would kick herself a hundred times, but tonight was for fun and this handsome man was in her bathroom and the fan blocked out all the noise from the party except for the faint thumping of the music.

"Kiss 'em," she blurted.

Michel raised an eyebrow, like her fifth-grade math teacher, and then chuckled.

"Well, I hope you do. But right now I need to use the little boys's room." He hung the hankie over the towel rack and pushed her out the door. As she headed upstairs to the party she thought how wonderful it was to flirt and be carefree again, even with somebody else's date.

"Try to stay out of trouble, eh?" Michel whispered in her ear as he made his way back out to the patio. Kara felt herself blush, but from the closeness of his breath in her ear and not his jibe. She was helping Annie prepare a new tray of munchies in the kitchen. If Annie noticed the intimate exchange, she kept her own counsel.

"You seem in high spirits tonight," she said.

"Well, it is quite a party," said Kara.

"It helps to have a handsome artist in attendance."

"Oh, you noticed that too," laughed Kara, "the handsome part, I mean."

"Every woman at this party has noticed."

"Mmm. Especially Chloe, I suppose."

"Yes, she's noticed, but only in relation to how it might make Jason jealous."

"Jason?" asked Kara, looking up from her tray of vegetables and dip.

"They were together almost a year, until last

month, that is. I think he started hearing wedding bells and panicked.''

Chloe and Jason? thought Kara. A whole year and she never knew about it. No wonder she had not seen Matthew's betrayal coming. The whole office had probably known about it before her.

Right then and there, as she arranged carrot sticks, she decided that it was time to make some changes. She had always left Annie to coordinate personnel and to deal with staff problems, but Matthew had scared her into a hole like a frightened rabbit. She had become too aloof. In-A-Wink could only suffer— had been suffering for it. She didn't want to dwell on the effects this detachment had on her own personal life, but at least she could control its effects on her company. First thing Monday morning she would call a staff meeting and assess her staff all over again. In the meantime, she would let them assess her. Maybe she could be one of the girls and still be the boss-lady. She picked up the platter and headed back out to the party.

As she put the tray on the picnic table, she realized how sensitive her staff really was to In-A-Wink's current problems. Jason, her unofficial top salesman since Matthew left, plunked another glass of punch in her hand and called out for everyone's attention.

''I'd like to make a toast,'' he said, ''to In-A-Wink's newest line, Prolar lenses. Monday is the big day. Michel is finally coming out of the closet with his packaging.'' There was a ripple of laughter.

Michel raised his glass to Jason, and when he caught Kara smiling at him, he winked.

"May we all work our bottoms off," continued Jason, "and show this industry some new standards of excellence. And I want to thank Kara for having enough courage for all of us to forge ahead with new and exciting projects like this one."

As the glasses were raised in her honor, Kara wondered: *Do they really think me courageous? Don't they see that it's an act of desperation?*

Whatever their private thoughts were, Jason's toast had put the guests in a congenial mood. Kara found herself, in the midst of a chattering crowd, feeling very much like one of the gang.

The longest day of the year was only a few days past, and at nine o'clock, the sun was still an orange glow in the west sky. Someone had lit the candle torches around the pool. Kara noted, with satisfaction, that everyone seemed content and at ease. The splashing and frolicking had ended, and people lounged on deck chairs, sipping their last drinks before heading to Ste. Helene's Island to watch the St. Jean Baptist fireworks. The candles were romantic, and most of the couples had split off from the main group to talk quietly at the small tables that Kara had strategically placed around the yard.

In less than a few hours Kara learned more about her staff than she had ever expected. She learned that Claude and his wife had a mentally handicapped daughter; Jeff, the accounts manager, was a closet tenor; Sherry, one of the secretaries, was engaged to be married, and the wedding was to take place as the bride and groom dangled from parachutes a thousand feet in the air.

Kara joked with Chloe about the men's selection of swim fashions and heard all about her latest breakup with Jason. She had never heard Chloe speak without her telephone voice. Suddenly Chloe didn't seem so perfectly feminine, and that was reassuring.

Kara knew that people spoke like this every day, but to her it was such a revelation. Would anybody go home tonight feeling as if they knew Kara MacKenzie any better? Though she drew out others, Kara didn't offer much information about her own life. Her most horrible secrets were public knowledge anyway, and she did not want to speak of them with anyone. But if she could continue, if she could bring herself to confide in her staff, to share her dreams for In-A-Wink, she knew that with this group of people they could again rise to number one. If they failed, though, this new intimacy would make next spring's layoffs even more painful.

Perhaps it was this lingering doubt that still made Kara hold back. Perhaps it was that she was incapable of truly letting go of her worries. Part of her still remained aloof, like a stranger watching with interest as this change took her over.

It was this separate part of her that was always aware of Michel. Whenever he refilled his glass, she knew. When he turned his back to her, she knew.

When his eyes bored into the back of her head, she knew. She envied those who animated his face with laughter and those who furrowed his brow in serious conversation. Kara did not speak to him all night.

Finally Michel stood by himself at the far end of the pool, and Kara was alone at the gate after saying goodnight to some guests. She felt a pang of guilt. She had pointedly ignored him all evening, pretending to herself that renewing acquaintances with her staff was more important. Michel did not seem the worse for her inattention. People naturally gravitated toward him. Even had Kara wanted his attention, she would have had to wait in line most of the night. And now, as the party wound down, he was alone, free to flirt with as she had so shamelessly done before.

Kara mumbled something about missed opportunities and walked some other guests to the driveway.

Jason and Chloe were speaking together quietly at the far end of the deck. They seemed to be in a world of their own, and Kara knew that it wouldn't be long before they edged out the gate to his car. She was happy for them. Jason had worked at In-A-Wink for many years, but she had never seen him act the clown as he had tonight. Apart from his antics with the pool toys, he had kept the energy level of the party going with his silly jokes and his hearty laughter. Chloe, though usually standoffish, had done her best to mingle with everybody. The point to this, of course, was to show Jason that she was independent and loving it, but it gave Kara the chance to know her a bit better.

"You two look cosy," said Kara, loud enough to interrupt their private talk.

"If we get any cosier we may never leave," said Jason with a smile.

"None of that talk," said Kara. "This old lady's got to get to bed soon."

"You're the youngest old lady I've ever met."

Kara smiled at the compliment. At least she didn't look as tired as she felt. She chatted with them some more, and then they, too decided to leave.

"Don't keep him out too late," Kara said to Chloe. "I need him in top shape Monday. We start the Prolar campaign."

"Don't worry," said Chloe, tugging on Jason's shirt sleeve. "I'll make sure he gets home early." With a sheepish grin, Jason let himself be dragged away.

Yow! thought Kara. *The true meaning of "nab yourself a man." Why don't I ever try that?*

Michel still leaned against the wall, sipping his drink. He had seen the exchange between Kara and the couple, but from his half-grin, she could not tell if he was amused or jealous.

"Another glass?" she asked, indicating the punch bowl. After the long afternoon, most people had already left, but she didn't want him to go.

"Looks like your date deserted you," said Kara.

"Yes, it seems that I have served my purpose. I do like a happy ending."

As usual, Kara could not tell if he was being sarcastic or not.

"So you knew that Chloe still cared for Jason?"

"Even if she hadn't told me the whole story already, I'd have to be blind not to have seen it."

"She told you all about her and Jason? How come I'm the only one who didn't know about it? I'm the boss, I'm supposed to know everything."

Michel laughed.

"Don't be upset," he said. "It's a myth that women tell other women everything. Really they only spill their guts to men. Believe me, I have many girlfriends."

"Oh you do, do you?"

Michel was startled at her sharpness.

"And just how many girlfriends are we talking? Like harem proportions, or can you count them on two hands?"

"My English still fails me sometimes," laughed Michel. "I must sound like some macho playboy. I don't mean girlfriends but rather girls that are friends. Of the first I have none. Of the second I have many. Models talk about themselves during the long hours of posing."

"Hmm," said Kara, unconvinced, "I bet they do. And how come these girls that are friends don't become girlfriends."

"I never date models. You get a bad reputation in the industry that way."

"Well there are plenty of pretty girls here," she

said, trying to change the subject in her own awkward way.

"Yes, there are," he said, meeting her eye. Once again, looking at him, she felt herself slipping away. She was falling for this man with the beautiful eyes and the gentle laugh, but she was unwilling and unable to let him know how much he affected her. How glad she would be when tomorrow came and went. After his contract was completed with In-A-Wink she could let her true feelings show, but she didn't fool herself into thinking that those feelings were in any way returned. Michel was as good as she was at being aloof. And though he had flirted with her on occasion, she knew that for a handsome man such as Michel, flirting must be second nature.

She tried to keep the conversation light. She asked him about his art. He told her about his hopes for his upcoming show at the Westmount Gallery, one of the finest in the city.

He asked her about In-A-Wink and she told him about their recent setbacks—leaving out the subject of Matthew—and her hopes for a good fall season.

The guests had been leaving by dribs and drabs until Kara looked around and realized that they were alone on the patio. From the kitchen she could hear the clanking of dishes and running water.

"Poor Annie!" said Kara rushing into the house. Annie always worked too hard. She had not even taken the time to enjoy the party, and now she was already busy cleaning up after it.

Kara burst into the kitchen with Michel in tow.

"Annie, stop that this instant!" said Kara in her sternest voice. Her assistant turned to see what the fuss was about. Her arms were into the soapy dishwater up to her elbows. "You are not expected to clean up all these dishes," continued Kara. "You've done more than enough."

"I won't leave you to clean this mess by yourself." Annie pointed at the mounds of clutter on every available counter.

"Nonsense," replied Kara. "Most of it is paper plates anyway."

"And I'll help with the rest," said Michel from the kitchen doorway.

Annie eyed first Kara then Michel.

"Well," she said, "if you wanted to be alone, you just had to say so."

Kara choked back a retort. Protesting would only make them look guiltier. She walked Annie to her car and said goodnight. There were no other cars in the driveway or the street. When she came back inside she asked Michel where his was parked.

He was pouring them each a glass of wine.

"I had no designed driver so I took a taxi. I hope you do not mind my helping myself." His speech was stilted again, and Kara wondered if he was uncomfortable being alone with her. He handed her a glass and said, "If we are going to tackle that mess, we need fortification."

"You don't really have to help me," said Kara, "I'll do it tomorrow."

"Oh, no!" said Michel. "If that old sergeant finds out I am a liar, I am done for!"

"Yes, Annie is a bit military," said Kara, refilling the sink, "but I'd be lost without her. Wash or dry?"

"Wash. You can put things away properly."

Kara tied the frilly apron around his waist, trying not to notice how close she was to touching him. He had slender hips and long legs. She resisted the urge to run her hands down his back. Over the lemony scent of dish soap, she could smell his spicy after-shave and, as always, the faint aroma of turpentine.

They worked in silence for a while, each absorbed with his or her own thoughts. Suddenly, out of the quiet, Michel remarked, "You know we have been chatting and flirting, and yet only now as we work in silence do I feel that I am getting to know the real Kara S. Mackenzie."

Kara flushed slightly when she realized that he had known she was flirting with him.

But that's silly, she thought, *He's not a little boy. Of course he would know. I wanted him to know.*

He was right about the silence, though. She felt a certain camaraderie with him as they worked. It was a feeling that she had never felt with anyone except Annie.

"You know," he said, "I only asked you out for lunch to apologize, not for a repeat performance."

"No need to apologize," Kara said quickly. She did not want to get into a debate about kissing ethics with this man. She knew where that would end.

"I would have loved to join you, but as you will

discover, under my frivolous facade I'm really a down-to-earth workaholic.''

''Well, you love your job. I can understand that. When you find yourself impassioned by something, it's easy to go overboard.'' His words spoke of work, but his eyes told her something else entirely.

Kara did not tell him that In-A-Wink was no longer her great passion. Something inside her was changing, and that made her wary. She felt the raw edge left by her fiancé's betrayal begin to heal under this man's gaze. Wounds may heal quickly, though, but the courage to do battle again took longer to regain. Reluctantly, she turned away from the charming scene of Michel—tall, broad shouldered, and clad in rubber gloves and frilly apron. Over the clamor of pots and pans, she asked, ''Is that how you feel about your work?''

''Yes,'' he said. ''It is a passion, but it's most certainly work.''

Kara thought it odd that he needed to justify himself like that, as if she might think that all artists were panhandlers. She let the unusual remark go without comment. How could she know what experiences had formed Michel? Perhaps, in the past, people had called him just that and worse.

''It sounds so exotic to me, mythical almost,'' she said. ''I can't even imagine what your life must be like.''

Michel just chuckled.

''You make it sound as if I have the Greek muses themselves as house guests. Believe me, it is anything but mythical. The world of art and artists is cutthroat and cynical.'' He stopped as if he wanted to say more, but thought better of it. ''Or maybe I am the cynical one. *Mon dieu,* I know I am cynical, but an artist by nature is also an optimist, always hoping that the next painting will be the masterpiece, that the next critic will not be a total ignoramus.''

Kara crouched to put some platters away under the counter. She stopped to listen, not wanting the clatter of dishes to interrupt him. As he scrubbed, he looked out the kitchen window, but his eyes saw much farther than the back yard. Kara didn't move from her crouch, afraid to break the spell.

''But when I get into my studio, I forget all that,'' he continued. ''There's only me, the paint, and the canvas. Strangest thing, a blank canvas. It has a certain odor, kind of ancient, like stone or marble. Have you ever smelled a canvas? It smells like death. Maybe that is why I am always so anxious to fill up the emptiness. The smell of paint is much more invigorating.''

For the first time he noticed Kara crouched at the cabinet. Embarrassed, she shoved the platters inside with a crash. Michel reached down with a soapy hand to help her up. They stood so close that the pleats of her skirt brushed against his apron.

''Have you ever smelled a blank canvas?'' he asked softly, and again, Kara felt that his words and his eyes were not asking the same thing. Was it only a trick of the light, or had the usual mocking glint in his eyes changed to something more tender?

"No, I haven't," she said, "but I'd like to. I'd like to see your studio."

His mouth, which had been slightly open as if ready to kiss her, clamped shut. His eyes, which had been gentle, hardened. He turned back to the sink and drained the murky water.

"My studio's always a mess," he said curtly. Kara stared at his back. She was certain that she had just been rebuked but didn't understand why. Had she been too forward? She wondered if maybe her eyes, too, spoke differently than her words. She was embarrassed that he thought she had propositioned him and then doubly embarrassed when she realized that he had turned her down.

"Maybe you would like to see the gallery, though," said Michel, as if in consolation, his back still to her.

Kara nodded, fighting back the ridiculous tears that were heating up her eyes. She was not a crier. Normally she faced her problems head on, without fear. She had not even cried at her father's funeral. Or after the Matthew fiasco. But Michel turned her emotions upside down.

They finished cleaning up in silence, but it was no longer companionable. On the front stoop they said goodnight. Kara could hardly believe that half an hour ago she had felt comfortable with this man. Now she couldn't even look at him. She folded her arms around her chest, just because they felt awkward at her side. She leaned against the closed front door and waited for him to take his leave. He had one foot down the steps, but he just stood there as if waiting for her to say something. The irrational sobs were still stuck in her throat and she said nothing.

"Kara . . . I . . ." He came back up the steps and stood in front of her. She still wouldn't look at him, afraid that if she saw those blue eyes again she would ask him to stay, and she already knew what his answer would be.

"I had a wonderful evening," he said, finally, and leaned over to kiss her on the cheek next to her mouth. His eyelashes brushed against her nose.

And then he was gone. She should have offered to drive him home or to call a cab, but she didn't. She watched him walk up the street toward a busy intersection. His strides were long and confident. She imagined that he whistled a tune. Long after he disappeared around the corner, Kara stood for a few minutes in the cool evening air. In the distance she could hear the fireworks at the St. Jean Baptist festival. All over the city people were celebrating in their own ways. She thought of Chloe and Jason and all the other lovers who were smooching in cars under the moonlight.

Even as she thought these silly, romantic thoughts, she knew it was only to take her mind off the burning sensation on her skin where Michel had kissed her. For days to come she would be dissecting that kiss. Was it a friendly kiss, a conciliatory kiss, or did its very placement, so close to her lips, suggest something more?

Chapter Four

Kara spent the rest of the weekend working in her garden during the day and on her promotional campaign at night. The coming season opened with Photokina. Held in Cologne, Germany, it was the largest trade show for the photographic industry. Distributors and manufacturers from all over the world came to present their wares to thousands of people. This year's show was more crucial than ever. Apart from her new lenses, she hoped to pick up the exclusive North American distributorship for a new gadget, something no other Canadian distributor could rival. She didn't know what it would be yet, but Photokina was sure to offer dozens of possibilities. Better still would be to find it before the show and, with the help of her new graphic artist—while she worked she insisted on thinking of Michel in that role, not letting herself slip into other more romantic thoughts—make a great package to show at Photokina. First she had to find that special gadget. It had to be something easy to sell, less than twenty dollars, useful, practical, and stylish. On Sunday she worked late into the night scanning trade magazines—not just photographic, but artistic, electronic, and anything else related to the field—to find that gadget. So far she had had no luck. The most interesting gadget she had seen was a waterproof film holder on a string.

Yahoo, she thought in disgust. *I'll just strike it rich with that.* She closed her magazine and turned off the light, but she knew that it would be many hours still before she would fall asleep. Her mind whirred with marketing strategies all aimed at the one thing that could save In-A-Wink: getting back many, if not all, of the accounts that she had lost to Matthew's defection. If that didn't happen by the end of Photokina, Kara would have to consider some serious downsizing, if not a complete shutdown. The thought appalled her so much that she still had not spoken of it to Annie.

Finally, as the sun was starting to lighten the sky, Kara dozed, but her sleep was disturbed by unusually vivid dreams in which she was trying to explain something to Michel, a paintbrush, and a canvas. Frustration brought her to the edge of tears as she couldn't make the brush paint the picture she wanted. When she woke up, a scant two hours later, she could not remember what it was she had been trying to explain. Michel's eyes had sparkled with humor and something else—pity?—as she had tried in vain to cover the canvas with her thoughts.

As tired as she was, she was glad to get up and let a cool shower wash away the night's anxieties.

She had promised herself to call a staff meeting first thing upon arriving at the office. Michel was there to present his mockups for the lens packaging, and he was included in the meeting. Kara was dressed in a proper suit with a fitted blazer, but her skirt was short and, as she sat on her desk with her legs crossed, her scarred knee visible to everyone. She felt somehow naked. She ignored Michel but could feel his eyes on her.

In her most efficient voice, she outlined every department's goals and made arrangements to meet each separately.

"I don't expect immediate results," she said trying to believe it herself. "Photokina is only the first step. I don't think any of you need to be told that this Christmas season is crucial to In-A-Wink's future."

There were a few muffled agreements, but none of the shocked silence she had expected from her implications.

Maybe I didn't make it clear exactly how grave the situation is, she thought. She was about to clarify herself, but then stopped. It was better that they not yet know the extent of the company's trouble.

As everyone shuffled out of the conference room, Kara asked Chloe to stay back a moment. Since Michel was going to present his mockups, he too stayed back.

"I hope everything is all right between you and

Jason,'' said Kara. For once the beautiful receptionist looked embarrassed, as if she were expecting a reprimand.

"Yes, a bit of fireworks did us good, I think." Kara smiled and touched her on the shoulder.

"I'm glad."

Chloe grinned and mumbled a thank-you before returning to her desk.

"That was gracious of you," said Michel when they were alone together.

"It think it's important that the staff knows that I'm okay about interoffice fraternization."

Especially after my own disastrous relationship with the chief of sales, she thought to herself.

Michel studied her with his head cocked to one side.

"What?" he asked, as if he was trying to listen to her thoughts.

"What do you mean?" she answered.

"You were going to qualify that statement with another, but you stopped yourself."

"Good heavens," she laughed. "It's bad enough that I already have Annie reading my mind, but not you, too!"

"Your expressions give you away. You would make a wonderful model," he said.

Kara just smiled and shook her head. She would not make the same mistake as she had Saturday night and assume that this was a proposition.

They sat at one end of the meeting table. The great expanse of mahogany dwarfed them. Without any words of introduction, Michel opened his portfolio case and laid out his drawings.

"What is the first color you see?" he asked.

"Yellow," she said, smiling as she remembered the same question from their outing at the old port. The package background was indeed yellow, but a muted mustard yellow with subtle shades of green and red swirled in. Scattered, collage fashion, were images of active people, biking, hiking, dressed up for the opera, or a polo match. All of the images spoke of class, style and excitement. Across the front of the box in bold letters was the lens name: Prolar.

A second sample replaced the hiking and biking pictures with macro images of colorful birds and flowers as well as closeups of insects and a silhouette of a couple on the beach at sunset.

"These images will all be photographs, not drawings," said Michel. "If we can't find them at an image bank, I know a good photographer."

Kara studied the drawings in silence. She was impressed with his work and was going to accept the samples right off, but she wanted him to believe that she deliberated over them. As she compared the subtleties of the background with the contrasting images, she knew she had done well to forgo the usual design routes. Michel had created a stunning effect. No other line could compete with it. Most packaging for lenses and accessories tended toward the functional not the artistic. In fact, she wouldn't be surprised if he had just started a new standard in the industry.

"Why did you do two samples?" she asked.

"Actually," he grinned sheepishly, "I did half a dozen." He pulled out a stack of rougher mockups from his case. Kara looked them over. They were done in different colors, blue, purple, and green. None of them had the impact of the yellow.

"I thought you could use this one," he said, indicating the sample with the hikers, "for the standard lenses, and the other for the macro lenses."

"I'm afraid we can't afford the production costs for two separate packages," said Kara. "We'll have to use the same for all the lenses. But maybe we could mix the images. Take out the polo match and the opera and replace it with the macro of the insect and the beach silhouette."

Kara smiled.

"Well," added Kara, "I'll think about it. We have a couple of weeks before it goes to final printing. For the rest, I'm really pleased. Once again, you've read my thoughts." Secretly she was a little apprehensive about the way he did that so easily. It made her feel vulnerable. "Can you work directly with the printer? I'll need final proofs by the end of the week."

"Should be no problem," he said, rising from the table.

Kara, too, stood and awkwardly extended her hand. Michel took it in both his own. He seemed to want to say something—something that had nothing to do with lenses or mockups. Instead he just thanked her and left.

Kara followed him into the reception. Chloe was busy with the flurry of morning phone calls. Kara noticed that her normal bored phone voice had been replaced by genuine friendliness.

Yes, she thought. *This just might be our best season yet.*

On Tuesday Annie brought Kara the mail, opened and sorted into bills, checks, letters, and junk. One of Kara's quirks was that she insisted on seeing everything, including the junk.

"You never know," she had once insisted to Annie. "The purchasing department might miss a good deal just because they're too busy to read the junk mail."

"And you're not too busy?" retorted Annie.

Still, In-A-Wink was not so huge that Kara couldn't go through every piece of mail in a few minutes, and it gave her a certain sense of control.

Today, however, she quickly put aside all the junk mail. Her eyes were drawn to a parchment envelope with fancy gold lettering.

"I thought you might be interested in that one," said Annie wryly.

"André-Guy Bernard," she read aloud, "cordially invites you to the opening of Michel Vernier's exhibit entitled '*La Loi*—The Law' at Westmount Gallery, Thursday, June 30, at 8:00 pm."

"That's this Thursday," said Annie.

Kara sighed and folded the invitation back into its envelope.

"I know," she said.

"You are going, aren't you?"

"I don't think he really wants me to."

"Don't be silly. Why would he send you an invitation then?"

Kara explained to her about the way she had, more or less, invited herself to Michel's studio and how he had, more or less, turned her down.

"It's more a consolation than an invitation," said Kara. "He didn't even mention it yesterday."

"I see," said Annie, pretending to be interested in tidying the files on Kara's desk. "So you are the only one allowed to have a past, are you?"

"What do you mean?"

"Kara, you are a shrewd businesswoman, but when it comes to romance you can be awfully thick."

Kara reddened, not at the insult but at the truthfulness of the statement.

"Has it not occurred to you," continued Annie, "that perhaps your offer—though not necessarily unwanted—was a bit forward?"

Kara had thought of that. In fact, she had spent Saturday night lying in bed thinking of nothing else.

"Have you also considered that maybe Michel too, has a painful past? That maybe he too, is still feeling the hurt from a recent relationship. Perhaps this invitation is not a consolation but a request that you take things more slowly."

"Did he tell you that?" asked Kara, "About the recent relationship, I mean."

"No, your friend is not the type to go on about his own troubles, but if I'm any judge of character—and I think I am—I tell you that artist of yours is not a happy man."

Kara considered this for a few minutes. Annie was right, of course. It was ridiculous to think that a man as handsome as Michel had no romantic past, but somehow, Kara could not imagine him on the hurting end of a breakup.

"Kara, dear," said Annie less severely, "not everyone is as easy to read as you. Give Michel a chance. Besides," her eyes twinkled with mischief, "a man who does dishes is nothing to sneeze at."

"Oh, go away!" said Kara with a laugh. Before Annie closed the door behind her, Kara knew she would be at the opening, even if she had to change around her schedule. She riffled through the files on her desk looking for her appointment book. It was a heavy black book with her initials embossed in gold on the cover. She remembered when Michel had asked her what they stood for.

Kiss 'em, she thought. *Oh, no! Did I really say that?* She vowed that when she saw him once more, not even his beautiful eyes would reduce her to such silliness again.

Chapter Five

" "Mademoiselle Mackenzie?" A thin, well-dressed man approached Kara. Being somewhat amazed by the throng of stylish people crowded into the small gallery, she hadn't noticed him until he spoke. Westmount was the hobnob hill in Montreal, but somehow she had not expected this lavishness. Waiters in tuxedos circled among the guests with glasses of champagne and dainty hors d'oeuvres. The gallery was well lit, and the only thing that stood out more than the cocktail dresses worn by the female guests were the paintings that hung on every wall. Kara resisted the urge to inspect them right away and turned to the thin man who had greeted her.

His expression was pinched, as if the bright lights in the gallery pained him. He did not extend a hand in greeting but kept both hands firmly in the pockets of his black slacks. One of the few men without a suit jacket, he wore a green silk shirt, open at the neck.

"Mademoiselle Mackenzie?" he repeated. "My name is André-Guy. I am the owner of Westmount Gallery and, you might say, Monsieur Vernier's agent. He is tied up in an interview at the moment and asked that I greet you. Would you like a soda?

Kara nodded, scanning the crowd for a glimpse of Michel. André-Guy handed her a glass and was about to turn away, but Kara stopped him. Despite the man's unfriendly air, she did not want to be alone in this strange crowd.

"This seems like a good turnout for a first showing," she said, making small talk.

"This is not Michel's first showing," replied André-Guy. "Only to the average person is he considered a newcomer in the art world."

Kara realized that, to the snooty André-Guy, she was painfully average. Not to be bullied, she asked a few more questions about the prospects of other shows and the critics' reviews so far. Though his answers were polite, André-Guy's bored manner made it plain that his duty to Kara was done and that he had more important matters to attend to. Kara made her way toward a group of admirers who stood in front of the largest tableau.

The show was entitled "The Law," and Kara had expected something totalitarian or military in style. Actually, she had had only vague imaginings—based mostly on her limited experience of art as well as Michel's mural at the office—of what his paintings would be like. Whatever she had expected, though, this was not it. The canvas was immense, ten by twelve feet, easily, and filled with a high angle view of a great waterfall, as if the observer was a bird, circling high above. The effect was so realistic that Kara was disoriented just looking at it. After blinking several times to erase the dizziness from her head, she noticed, in the bottom right corner, a small figure—man or woman, she could not tell—climbing the face of the rock beside the spray of the falls.

Kara didn't understand what this had to do with law, unless he meant the law of gravity, but as she studied more of his works throughout the gallery, she realized that he meant the law of nature. Each canvas depicted a power of nature—lightning, sandstorm, two bucks clashing in combat—and in each there was a lone figure, neither man nor woman, but simply a spectator, or perhaps a judge to the law.

Kara felt herself become excited by the raw energy in the paintings. Under that strength she also sensed a melancholy, portrayed by the lone figures. Kara's heart went out to the man who had painted them. Annie was right as usual; beneath Michel's easy manner there was a deep hidden sadness. Not for the first time, Kara thought that the man she had so easily flirted with was more complex than any she had ever known.

''Do you not like them?'' a deep voice said in her ear. She turned to face Michel's mocking grin. He looked so boyish and playful that it was hard to reconcile him with the artist of these dark paintings. The intensity in his eyes was not flirtation but a passion of an altogether different kind. It was a passion reflected in his work. She wondered what it was like for him to see all these people gathered for the sole purpose of admiring and criticizing that passion.

"I . . . I like them very much," said Kara. Michel narrowed his gaze at her in disbelief. "No, really. I do. It's just not what I expected."

"And what did you expect?"

"Honestly, I don't know. This is all so beyond my realm of experience. But I am pleasantly surprised."

Michael seemed satisfied with her response.

"Thank you." He squeezed her hand. "Your approval means more to me than these critics." He took her empty glass and replaced it with a full one from the tray of a passing waiter. As they wandered around the gallery, Kara wanted to ask him about his inspiration for the paintings, but they were continually interrupted by fans and critics. Finally, a reporter from the *Montreal Gazette* asked for an interview.

"I am sorry, Kara," he said, "but duty calls. Will you be all right?"

Kara nodded. She didn't want him to go just yet, but she knew that she had no right to ask him to stay. This was his big night. Michel kissed her on the cheek, again, just beside her mouth, as if that was where his lips really wanted to go.

As he walked away, Kara noticed how pretty the reporter was, and the way she leaned into him as if he spoke too softly. Michel laughed at something she said, and Kara turned away. She put her half-finished glass down and did not take another.

The rest of the evening dragged on. Twice Kara tried to get Michel's attention, but he was busy with his admirers. Once, Michel saw her watching him from across the room. He smiled and tipped and an imaginary hat in her direction, but made no move to go to her.

Finally, when Kara had absorbed all of the paintings, to the point where a few were permanently etched on her memory, she left. She tried to signal to Michel that she was going, but he seemed oblivious to everything except the group of people around him. Kara couldn't help noticing that the pretty reporter was among them. André-Guy seemed to see Kara's hand signal, but he ignored her and led Michel off in the opposite direction to meet a late-arriving guest.

Kara had not noticed how chilly the gallery's air conditioning had been until she stepped out into the warm evening. She sat in her parked car in the dark lot without touching the ignition. She leaned back on the headrest and closed her eyes. Her cheek still tingled where he had kissed her, so agonizingly close to her mouth.

Why does he always bring me so close, she thought, *if only to push me away?*

His world was strange to her: the cold agent, the posh customers, the eager critics, and above all, those passionate, heart-rending paintings. She was used to men in blue three-piece suits carrying attaché cases. She knew, to her chagrin, that her jealous reaction had as much to do with her alienation as it did with the pretty reporter.

I'm sure I could get over the strangeness, she thought, *but that fawning reporter is another matter.*

She was already thinking of them as a couple, as if Michel had expressed his desire to be with her when, of course, he hadn't. She put the car in gear and maneuvered her way out of the cramped parking lot, glad to be away from André-Guy's gallery.

Early the next day, the remorse set in. Kara began to wonder if she had been too rash. It was Michel's big opening night, after all, and he did have certain obligations. It was not as if he had asked her on a date or anything. What if he was even insulted that she had left so early?

She picked up the phone and put it down again, not knowing his number. She could look it up, but that would mean asking Annie for the directory. Somehow, she knew that Annie would guess whom she was calling.

She picked up the phone again and dialed information. Luckily, the operator did not ask for his street address because she did not know that either. There must have been only one Michel Vernier in the Greater Montreal area.

"Hello?" He picked up the line after five rings, stretching Kara's nerves to the limit.

He sounded distracted, and Kara wondered if he was alone.

"Um, Michel?" Her voice was girlish.

"Kara!" Suddenly she had his full attention. "I was hoping you would call. I am very sorry about last night."

"You're sorry?" asked Kara. His voice was beginning to sound familiar to her ears. She could even imagine the worried crease in his brow.

"Stop frowning," she said, "or you'll get wrinkles."

Michel laughed. The carefree sound sent a shiver along Kara's spine. He seemed in high spirits. The show must have been a success.

"I shouldn't have left so early," she continued, "but . . . I don't know. I felt out of my element."

"Don't apologize," he said. "If I could have, I would have left with you."

There was an awkward pause as each of them considered the implications of his last remark.

"Would you meet me for dinner?" Kara asked. As soon as the words were out, Kara wondered if, once again she had been too forward. Would Michel throw up a wall between them again?

"How about Thursday night?" he asked, surprising her with his casualness. "I'll meet you at the Claremont Cafe. It's on Sherbrooke West . . ."

"I know where it is," said Kara. Claremont was where Kara often took prospective clients for a bit of Montreal's night life.

"Good," said Michel. "I'll meet you there at seven. You can tell me what you really thought of the show."

The show! Only after she hung up did Kara realize

that she had not even offered an opinion on his opening. Not one encouraging word.

She made a mental note to make it up to him Thursday night.

Cafe Claremont was a small restaurant in Montreal's west end that catered to an assortment of young professionals, artists, and students. It was far enough outside the city center to be overlooked by tourists. At seven in the evening the music was loud enough to compete with the passing traffic. The sidewalk terrace was full, and a short line had already appeared at the door. Kara hoped that Michel was already inside, or they would have to wait.

Avoiding the lineup, Kara pushed her way through the terrace and went in through the sliding doors. Michel was waiting for her at a small table beside the bar. As she approached him, he stood up to greet her. He wore a gray crew-neck shirt with a darker gray vest and pants. He seemed as comfortable in these stylish clothes as he had in his paint-stained smock. He moved with a grace that spoke of class and self-confidence. His eyes brought the gray of his attire alive, and for the first time she noticed, not the crazy eyelashes, but the crinkled crow's feet at the edges. He might have some hidden sadness, but still, Michel Vernier was a man who laughed easily.

''You look great,'' he said, kissing her cheek in a friendly way. Kara resisted the urge to fluff her hair. She had spent more time than usual preening in front of the mirror this evening. She had changed her outfit four times before settling on a one-piece linen dress in cream. She knew that the earth tone brought out the red highlights in her hair, and so she had left it long, down her back.

Kara watched Michel surreptitiously. He was a handsome man, no doubt about it, but his character was fraught with inconsistencies. He had a full, sensual mouth, and when he smiled she noticed that one of his teeth was chipped. His hair was combed neatly away from his face in waves, and yet there was always one unruly curl that stuck out from his right temple, a cowlick that would not be tamed.

His manner was also contradictory. They chatted about the people from Kara's office. Michel's soft voice easily carried over the noise and the music. His eyes never left her face and yet, he seemed to lean back, away from her.

He did laugh easily. She told him the story about how she had caught two of her staff kissing in her office.

"Next to my desk!" she said feigning shock.

"And did you fire them?"

"No, the lights were off. I pretended to be the cleaning lady, excused myself, and left. I was so anxious to get out of there that I tripped over a wastepaper basket and made a horrendous noise."

Michel's laugh was deep and infectious.

"I'm a bit of a klutz, in case you hadn't already noticed." She said it ruefully, but she was not embarrassed. Kara was not a social butterfly, but she had always enjoyed making people laugh. She told stories and sang silly songs. Only Matthew had been immune to her sense of humor. She never had seen him crack more than a begrudging grin.

Kara knew than it was not a good idea to compare Michel and Matthew in her mind. Michel would only come out ahead, and he was already far too attractive. Still, it warmed her heart to know that she could amuse him.

In the lull, Michel said, "I would have let them know it was me."

"Hmm," mumbled Kara, "I should have, but honestly, I'm not the best role model for interoffice fraternization. I was engaged to my top salesman."

Michel raised an eyebrow but said nothing.

"We broke up last fall."

When Kara didn't seem to be offering any more details, Michel scanned his menu. She had not meant to talk about Matthew and somehow, it being said, she felt like his ghost hung in the air between them. She looked at her menu for five minutes without reading a word. The waiter returned, but Kara was not yet ready to order.

Michel ordered some appetizers.

"We'll start with that and you can decide later," he said, taking the menu from her hand.

"I didn't take you for the Claremont Cafe type," said Kara, trying to recover the easy small talk.

"Why not?"

"Well, all this," she said, pointing a the gaudy abstract painting that hung on the wall behind him. Claremont was famous for showing local art, but sometimes Kara thought that they went for shock value instead of artistic virtue.

"All this," she repeated. "I don't know. You just seem so beyond it."

"Actually, I had my first public showing here." He smiled at her embarrassment. "Don't worry, it was pretty rotten stuff too."

"I guess I just don't understand art," she said with a sigh.

"No, you understand it just fine," said Michel. "You know what you like, and this"—he pointed at the glaring canvas of purple and green splotches behind him—"is not it. Can't say I blame you either." He took a sip of his drink.

"I wish everyone understood art the way you do," he continued. "The others are the ones who don't get it."

"Who?" asked Kara.

"Them." He nodded toward the hip-looking crowd that milled around the bar. "And all the masses who are too shy to have an opinion. They think that just because it's hanging on a wall it's great art. No wonder we artists have such fragile egos. We can never trust our audience."

"So why do you come here?" asked Kara.

"The food's great," he said with a smile as he speared a seafood springroll from the platter that had just been unceremoniously dumped on their table.

Kara was intrigued by his little outburst and liked that he felt strongly about things that mattered.

"I wanted to tell you that your show was really

fantastic,'' she said, ''or at least that I thought so.''
She blushed at her own arrogance. To him she must
seem like one of the mass of uneducated art critic
wannabees, but he only smiled and said, ''Thanks.''

''And again, I'm sorry for sneaking out like that,''
continued Kara, ''but I just felt so uncomfortable.
Almost like that lone figure in each of your
paintings.''

''Uncomfortable?'' said Michel, frowning. ''You
see him like that?''

''Actually,'' said Kara, forgetting her shyness. ''I
didn't see him as a 'him' at all. More androgynous,
anonymous, but certainly uncomfortable. And
lonely.''

''I never looked at it that way,'' said Michel. ''I
thought of him as more of a witness. You know the
old cliché—if a tree falls in the forest and nobody
hears it, did it really fall? Well the figure is the witness to validate the laws of the earth. But I suppose,
you're right, by his very nature, a witness is a soli-
tary soul.''

He smiled and raised his glass.

''To you, Kara. Just as I thought I had myself
together, you come along to show me that I still have
a long road ahead.'' He clinked his glass against
hers. Kara had a feeling that his words held some
double meaning. Just as she was about to question
him, she noticed Matthew pushing his way through
the crowded tables toward them.

''Darn!'' swore Kara.

''What?'' said Michel. ''I was only kidding . . .''

"No, not that." She pretended not to notice Matthew. She took Michel's hand in hers, hoping that Matthew would not interrupt a seemingly intimate moment.

"That ex-fiancé that I mentioned?" Michel nodded. "He's about three tables away and closing fast."

"Hello, Kara." Matthew was dressed, as usual, in a suit and tie. Not only was he not embarrassed to have interrupted them, Kara could tell by his gloating smile that he was actually pleased. He stood with his back turned slightly toward Michel, as if to dismiss him.

"Fancy meeting you here," he said. Kara had forgotten the way Matthew spoke in clichés.

"I see you're looking as spiffy as ever," she said, keeping her tone light.

"Well, you know, old habits die hard." He continued to focus on Kara, but Michel had an aura of authority that could not be ignored. When Matthew made an unconscious turn toward him, Kara introduced the two men. Matthew narrowed his eyes slightly as they shook hands but seemed otherwise unmoved.

"Haven't seen you around the old watering hole lately," said Matthew.

"I've been busy." Kara sounded curt. More than anything, she didn't want Matthew to have the satisfaction of seeing her rattled, so she added, "Been getting ready for Photokina. Will you be there?"

Anyone who was anyone in the photo industry

showed up at Photokina. Matthew understood her slight in suggesting that he might not be there.

"Yes, of course," he said, frowning. "I wouldn't miss it." Then he brightened up and pointed to the pretty blond woman across the restaurant at his table. "My fans would never forgive me."

Kara felt her stomach clench when she recognized the woman, not because she was beautiful—which she was—and not because Kara was jealous—which she was not—but because the woman was Brenda Rosen, owner of a chain of photo stores in Montreal, and a faithful client of In-A-Wink. Rosen had been one of the first to invest in the company when Kara was just a one-woman show. Kara had hoped that they shared a special bond, being two women in a male-dominated industry, but she doubted that bond would withstand Matthew's lies.

Kara knew that her pause betrayed her shock.

"I believe you know my lovely date," flaunted Matthew. Kara could feel the anger burbling up from the depths of her gut. She wished she had the presence of mind to hold it back, but one look at Matthew's smirking face and it all spilled over.

"Don't flatter yourself, Matthew. I may have been stupid enough to fall for your fake charm, but you're way out of your league here. You have neither the wit nor the money to keep Brenda Rosen's attention past an order of hors d'oeuvres."

Matthew's expression darkened.

"Maybe not," he said, "but without your narrow-minded stinginess at my back, you can be sure that when she does place an order, it will be much more than just hors d'oeuvres. Nothing like small-time In-A-Wink ever saw.''

''Oh, Matthew, get over it. What's done is done. Move on already!'' Kara willed her voice to be steady. She waved her fingers at him, as if to dismiss a troublesome child, and turned her attention back to Michel, who watched the bizarre exchange with interest.

Matthew leaned down, forcing Kara to look him in the eye.

''No, Kara. It's not done yet.'' He pushed himself roughly back through the crowd to his table.

''Wow,'' said Michel. ''Want to tell me what that was all about?''

Kara knew, just by his expression, that should she wish it, Michel would not press her. Somehow, knowing this made her want to tell him all the more.

''Okay, but not here.'' She had to get away, before Matthew put a few drinks in him and decided to butt heads again. As they left, Kara suggested that they take a taxi downtown, but Michel said he would drive her car, to give her time to collect herself. Kara nodded. The taxi suggestion had just been an attempt to gain back an ordinary feeling to the evening, small talk to calm her rattled nerves.

Instead of driving east, toward the city center, Michel headed west. They drove through the suburbs in silence. Kara didn't ask where they were going. She laid her head back and closed her eyes. Her temples throbbed. Matthew was still able to make her grit her teeth in anger. A riot of images—arguments, embarrassments, hurts—played out in her head like a fragmented nightmare. She trusted that whenever they arrived at their destination, and she began to tell her story, that the images would find an order of their own.

Eventually, they pulled up a long driveway in front of a white stone house.

"Where are we?" asked Kara.

"Senneville," replied Michel. "The family manor."

Kara had never been to the posh suburb on the river, but she had heard that even the smallest of Senneville's houses were mansions by most standards.

The rumors are true, thought Kara, *if this place is anything to judge by.*

Michel led her through the house without turning on any lights.

"You can see all this later," he said. "I want to show you something really terrific."

They made a pit stop in the kitchen to refuel with some munchies: grapes, crackers, and cheese.

"This way," he said, leading her out the back door. The night was still warm and lit with a soft glow by an almost full moon. Kara's shoes were quickly wet with dew. She took them off and gasped at the shock of cold grass on her feet.

"Are you afraid of the dark?" teased Michel.

"A little," said Kara, playing along. "Will you protect me from the wolves?"

"Uh-huh." He flung his arm over her shoulder.

"How about the demons and boogeymen?"

"Demons, yes, but boogeymen? No way. You're on your own there."

"Okay, it's a deal." Once again, Michel had made her feel at ease. Matthew's vicious smirk seemed a lot father than just a few miles away.

He led her through the trees until they came to a clearing. A small creek burbled past a knoll. On top of the hill was a gabled gazebo.

"It's a fairy hill!" cried Kara.

"Fairy hill?" asked Michel with a frown.

"Yes, like in the old tales. The fairies live under the hill and on full moons they come out to dance on top of it."

"Yes, I'm aware of the stories," said Michel, still frowning. Kara wondered if she had said something wrong again. But then he brightened and added, "But I'm sure that we'll have it all to ourselves tonight."

They climbed the hill and settled into the wicker love seat in the gazebo.

"It is magical," said Kara. The rippling sound of the creek was like romantic music in the background. "You really grew up here?"

"Hmm. It wasn't always magical, but this fairy hill, as you call it, has been a special place for me. I used to come here after . . . well, when I needed some time out. At the cafe I saw your hands shaking, and I knew that you needed a time-out, too."

Kara nodded. It had finally come. If she didn't

speak about Matthew now, she never would. Everybody—her family, friends, employees—knew about their engagement and subsequent breakup, but Kara herself had never spoken about it to anyone. By opening up to this man, she knew she was committing herself. Already she found him stimulating, but she knew that by bringing her here and prodding her gently to open up, he had also become her friend.

His fingers touched hers. They were artist's fingers, competent and sensual. She looked up into his face and saw him watching her. The shadow fell across him, but his eyes were almost luminous in the dark. He leaned toward her, as if to kiss her, but instead, he handed her a glass and then physically turned her so that, with his arm around her shoulder, she leaned back on his chest. The movement was so deft, that she was settled in comfortably before she could resist. He seemed to understand that excitement would stop her from speaking, and though he had pulled her against him, he did not touch her. One arm lay across the top of the couch while the other held his glass.

''Now tell me.'' His voice, just a whisper in her ear, was too soft to be insisting. His lips lingered near her ear, as if he was taking in the scent of her hair, but he did not kiss her. It was easier for Kara to concentrate without having to look at the intensity of his eyes.

''Matthew asked me to marry him last year at our staff party.'' Kara's voice sounded unnaturally loud, as if she were back at that party, trying to speak over all the noise.

They had had many reasons to celebrate that night. The spring Photo Marketing Association show had been a great success. Matthew had landed two major new accounts. Riding high on his success, as well as several drinks, he had decided to take the plunge.

The party had been at a small Italian restaurant that Kara and Matthew had often frequented. The owner, Antonio, and his wife, Maude, were almost like family. Once a year, they closed the restaurant to the public for In-A-Wink's rambunctious staff party.

After the main course, Matthew stood up and banged his fork on his glass to get everyone's attention.

"With Antonio's help," he said, "I have an announcement." With great ceremony, Antonio served Kara with a parfait dish of raspberries and whipped cream. Sitting atop the cream was a diamond engagement ring.

"It's his words that I remember most," said Kara, half turning to see if Michel was paying attention to the story. He nodded for her to continue. " 'I have an announcement,' he said, as if I was another new account that he had brought in. He just assumed that I would say yes! Of course, I would have anyway, but somehow, with all those eyes staring at me . . . all my employees, Tony and Maude looking on like loving parents . . . for an instant, I wanted to say no. I wanted to scream it."

The memories agitated her. She fidgeted in her seat, chafing against Michel. He stroked her long hair as if she were a little girl, just awakened from a nightmare.

"So you said yes." Michel's voice was gentle, urging her on. Kara nodded and slumped against him. His chest was firm and comforting against her back. Suddenly, she became aware of his fingers running through her hair. This was the first time she had been so close to him. Strangely, all the anxiety ebbed from her.

"I was a foolish woman," she continued. "I never felt good about our relationship after that. I constantly looked for problems, for reasons not to go through with it."

"You must have found one." Michel's hands left her hair to gently massage her slender neck.

"Did I ever."

They were supposed to be married in the fall, but Kara had put it off, saying that the Christmas buying season needed her full attention. Matthew complained that there would never be a good time.

"Let's just go ahead and get married," he said. "Forget about all the trappings of a church wedding. We'll just go away and do it."

"My mother would never forgive us."

"It would serve the old witch right," sneered Matthew. "She'll drive you crazy with all this wedding business anyway."

Matthew never hid his dislike for Monica, and though they argued about many things, Kara couldn't fault him for that. There were times when she didn't like Monica either. She wished, however, that he wasn't so verbal about his opinions. She said as much, knowing, as she opened her mouth, that she was picking a fight.

By the end of the summer, they were arguing constantly and it carried over into the workplace. Kara noticed a definite drop in office morale. The staff arrived late in the morning and left early in the afternoon. Kara was too wrapped up in her own problems to reprimand them. She left the running of the office entirely to Annie, who was already overwhelmed with her own duties. Important projects were left to the last minute and then finished sloppily, and the staff just didn't get along like a team.

One afternoon, while Kara sat in her office brooding about her last evening with Matthew, she heard the girls in the secretarial pool arguing. For the first time, her head came out of her own self-imposed fog. She realized how her attitude, and Matthew's, colored the office atmosphere. She decided that enough was enough, and went to confront him, to talk things out and make them better.

The door to his office was slightly ajar, and as she approached, she could hear that he was on the telephone. She almost turned away, but his words stopped her.

''I'm telling you, Barry, Kara doesn't know what she's doing,'' he said to his brother, their lawyer, on the other end. Kara was rooted to the spot. ''Believe me, it's for the best. If I don't take over soon, the company will be in ruin. I give it two years.'' There was a pause while Matthew listened to his brother's response. Kara's cheeks were aflame.

How dare he? This was worse than if she had caught him with another woman. Kara sometimes wished that Matthew would have an affair, if only so that she could have an excuse to end things. But this! Kara realized that Matthew's lusts ran in a different direction, and he would never be so foolish as to ruin his perfect little nest. This was the masterpiece of betrayals.

''Don't worry,'' Matthew continued. ''She won't even notice the shift. She'll be so busy with babies that it will be only natural for me to take over.'' Another pause. Kara's rage gained steam. They had spoken about family, but Kara had made it clear that she would continue to run In-A-Wink. The company was, in a way, her firstborn. All the while Matthew had agreed with her, only to placate her into a false sense of independence.

''Yes, yes. We'll get it in writing, but not yet. She's not ready.''

So Barry is going along with it, she thought. *Just perfect.*

Kara had heard enough. She pushed open the door. She was hurt and afraid of the confrontation that she had come looking for, but anger overrode all those emotions and propelled her forward. Matthew saw her standing in his doorway, her eyes blazing.

"Uh, Barry, I'll call you back." He hung up the phone. "Kara . . ."

"How dare you?" she said. Her voice was void of the emotions that threatened to choke her. "You sit there and play president. You don't own this company and you never will!"

"Kara listen to me . . ." He smiled ingratiatingly, placating.

"No you listen, and listen well. In-A-Wink is my baby and I will do anything to keep it. Now get out."

"You can't fire me," he sneered. "I have a contract. I own enough shares . . ."

"Read the fine print, Matthew. It may cost me a bundle to buy you out, but it will be worth every penny. Don't bother collecting your things. I'll have them sent along. Just get out." Saying the words felt good. She wanted to repeat them over and over like a jumprope ditty: Get out, Matthew. Get out. They stared at each other across the desk for several moments. Kara was aware of the silence in the reception behind them. The whole office had stopped to hear the battle. She wondered who they rooted for.

"Fine," Matthew said, finally, "you fired me. I want it in writing." His back was against the wall. "There's no way that I'll let you twist this to make it look like I quit. I want my due."

"You'll get it," said Kara through gritted teeth. "And your written proof, as soon as my new lawyer draws it up."

"Now, Kara." He banged his fist on the desk. "I

want it now, before I leave this office." A crowd had gathered around his open door.

Kara lowered her voice, fighting to keep her cool.

"By law, I have five days to complete your leaving papers. They will be mailed to you."

"Now, Kara," he repeated. "I'm not leaving here without them." With a sickening smirk, he sat down and propped his feet on his desk. "Without those papers, I am still in control here."

Control? For a moment Kara wondered at his sanity. This all seemed like a big game to him. She looked around his office and, for the first time, she realized how sloppy he really was. There were stacks of files everywhere, sample products lay about haphazardly, and bits of paper with scribbled notes littered the floor. She had a suspicion that Matthew's performance was due more to the hard work from the junior staff than to his own efforts. She had a brief image in her mind of In-A-Wink under his disorganized direction. Inwardly, she cringed. Matthew still smirked at her. His hands rested casually behind his head to support his inflated ego.

Without another word, Kara pushed through the crowd and headed for the reception desk.

"Chloe, please call security and have them remove Mr. Richmond from our office. He doesn't seem to understand that he has been fired."

Chloe's usual poise was gone. She nodded awkwardly and dialed the building security with trembling fingers. As Kara headed back to her own office, she heard Matthew's whoop of laughter and, once again, questioned his sanity.

"He wants you to call security," said Annie. She brought Kara a mug of strong black coffee. They left the door open so that they could hear Matthew rant and rave across the office. Kara noted with grim satisfaction that none of the staff seemed to rally to his side.

"He needs to prove that you kicked him out so that you don't try and cheat him out of his severance."

"I know," said Kara, "but the money's not important. I just want him out."

"I hope that you'll be saying that in six months' time."

They sat quietly for several minutes, listening to Matthew slander Kara to the staff. Even so, the anger was draining from her. He seemed more pathetic than anything else.

"It's so easy for him to believe the worst of me," said Kara.

"That's because if the roles were reversed," said Annie, "he would be sure to betray you." That was the first and last time that Annie ever spoke badly of Matthew, a fact that made her words ring with truth. Kara thought back to all the nasty things Matthew had said about Annie, and felt a great relief that she had turned away from disaster.

"Oh, Annie! What have I done?" Always in tune, Annie knew that Kara did not fret about this morning's decision, but rather, about the two wasted years that she had spent with Matthew.

"You did what any young woman would have done faced with his charm, but today you acted with a courage that few could have mustered. I'm proud of you, Kara, and as soon as he's out of here, you will be, too."

When security arrived, Matthew politely shook everybody's hand—except for Kara and Annie—telling them each what a pleasure it had been working with them. He donned his coat, picked up his briefcase, and left.

"I was just glad that it was over," Kara said to Michel.

"I can imagine." He had been very still, listening to her strange tale. A slight wind blew up, rustling the oak trees in tune with the river.

"But I knew that the aftershock was far from over. I wanted to fire the whole staff right then and there, as if they had been tainted by the experience."

"Rather than go through the embarrassment of having to face them," said Michel. They were tough words, and not a question, but said with a kind voice as if he knew how it felt to want to hide from the world.

Kara nodded.

"It wasn't the staff's fault, though. I couldn't punish them for my own foolishness."

"You weren't foolish. There was no way you could have known."

"But that's the worst part. I did know. I was ready

to marry a man that I didn't love. I was ready to settle for comfort instead, but subconsciously I knew something wasn't right. I used to dream of other men kissing me or about walking out on Matthew, and yet I let it go on so long. I almost married a creep.''

"Because you didn't know any better," said Michel. He held her close against him and whispered in her ear. "But now you do."

"Yes, now I do."

They sat quietly for a few moments just enjoying the closeness. Kara felt better after telling her story. It seemed just that, now: a story.

"Do me a favor, Michel?"

"Mmm?" His voice was a low rumble.

"If you ever ask a girl to marry you, do it in private."

"I'll remember that." He took her glass away and put it on the floor. "You know what bothers me the most?" he asked. Kara turned slightly in the love seat to face him. "It bothers me that such a loving woman would willingly settle for less than love." He weaved her fingers in with his own and looked her in the eyes. The moon had shifted enough so that they were no longer in shadow. The faint glow picked up the shine in her hair. Her eyes were bright with unshed tears.

"You are a beautiful thing," he said. His English, usually flawless, was stilted. He brushed a bit of hair away from her mouth and kissed her.

Kara had known it was coming, but when his lips touched hers, she felt herself fall away into the spiraling blackness. The rest of her body ceased to exist, only her lips on his. It was a long drink of water after many dry months. With his fingers, he caressed her neck, her temples, the soft spot behind her ear. Kara's head stopped spinning and she opened her eyes to find him staring at her.

He stared at her with an intensity that was only exaggerated by the thick lashes that shadowed his eyes. The coil that had been wound tightly in Kara's gut snapped. Michel pushed himself away and asked, ''More sparkling water?''

Kara nodded, a little confused. When he stood up to get the bottle she went and leaned against the railing and looked out at the river. Suddenly the burbling water was no longer music, and the fairy hill was just a hill. Even the moon seemed smaller. She crossed her arms over her chest in defense of the cold.

''Don't do that,'' said Michel, coming up from behind her.

''Do what.''

''Stand with your back to me and your arms crossed against your chest as if to keep the whole world out.''

''I'm cold,'' she said, but then she turned toward him. She would not let this evening end in confusion again. She would not let him play games with her.

''You pulled away first,'' she said. ''You always do.''

Michel put his arms around her. His lips buried deep in her hair.

"Oh, Kara." He breathed in the scent of her. "Always the paradox. A self-assured businesswoman one minute, a little girl the next."

Kara did not respond, but only listened, hoping that his words would soothe the ache inside her.

"Don't you know how easy it is to get close to you?" asked Michel. He cupped her face in his hands and made her look up at him. "How easy it is to kiss you and hold you? When we get closer, I don't want it to be because you are too upset by your past to make the right decision."

I'm not upset, thought Kara, but she didn't say it aloud. Tomorrow, when she was away from the heat of his embrace and the scent of his cologne, she would be grateful.

Right now, though, she wanted to kiss him again.

"I guess I'd better go, then. Do you want a lift back to town for your car?"

He shook his head.

"Kara, please don't be angry."

"I'm not angry. I'm . . . I don't know what I'm feeling. Embarrassed, I guess, and a little grateful." She smiled ruefully.

He wrapped his arms around her and they stared out at the night for several minutes. Next to the heat of his body, she was cold, and she relaxed into his warmth. Now that they had confronted the tension between them, she found that she could enjoy this closeness. This kind painter had made her mind whirl, but still this closeness felt so right, like nothing she had ever felt before.

When he finally let her go, the night seemed chilly. They walked hand-in-hand back through the woods. They kissed again on the gravel driveway, as she stood in the open door of her car.

''Will you be able to get home all right?'' asked Michel.

''I figure if I just head east, I'm bound to hit the city eventually.'' She smiled at him and touched his face. One day she would spend an hour just tracing her finger along those dimples that shaped his mouth. And she was happy enough to think of that one day.

Chapter Six

The next week went by slowly at the office. Photokina was just two months away, but Kara could not motivate herself to work on the booth. The fall buying season had not yet begun, and the phones were quiet. She had spent two days going over Christmas projections, and they didn't look good.

She did not speak to Annie about her encounter with Matthew, preferring to bear the brunt of her worries alone.

In the afternoon lulls, Kara resisted the urge to call Michel. They spoke to each other each evening, chitchatting and teasing, but neither had suggested that they meet again. Michel was busy on new canvases. His show at Westmount had been a success, and he had been invited to New York, but he didn't have enough paintings completed for another show.

By the end of the week Kara decided that she had better put her restless energy to good use or she would go mad. In the past year she had discovered that her misgivings about Matthew riding on the hard work of the junior salespeople had been correct. After he left, the staff began airing their grievances, and Kara had heard an earful. Apparently Matthew had never kept his opinions of Kara's business skills a secret, which explained why he had been so careless in letting her overhear.

Kara wished that she had some contact close to Matthew, someone who could confirm or deny her suspicions that Matthew was plotting something against In-A-Wink. She thought of calling Brenda Rosen. Matthew had probably regaled her with tales of Kara's incompetence, but he might have also, in his arrogance, let slip some of his own plans. If only she could trust Brenda not to turn around and call Matthew. The last thing Kara wanted was for Matthew to think that he had her on the run. She was down, but not yet out of the game.

Unfortunately, Matthew had—out of desperation—promised the world to his new employer, and he had found the will to deliver a good chunk of it. In-A-Wink had suffered the effects. Photokina was their chance to get back a lot of that business. Friday afternoon she decided to call a staff meeting to start planning their booth. Nobody actually worked on Fridays anyway.

Sitting around the mahogany table in her office, she discussed aggressive pricing strategies with accounting, marketing tools with advertising, and new leads with sales. Still it would take more than this to entice back lost clients.

"We need something really big," said Kara, chewing on the end of her pencil. "Something to stir up media attention." The room was silent, each person absorbed in his own thoughts. Kara flipped through some European photo magazines still absently searching for that elusive gadget that the public would snatch off the shelf. Just as something caught her eye, Jason cleared his throat.

"Why don't you have Michel design the booth?" he asked.

"Michel?" asked Kara, looking up from her magazine.

"Yes, the painter, you know . . ." He pointed at the Prolar mockups on the table.

"I know who you mean," Kara said brusquely. It was a fabulous idea, but did she dare?

"He could recreate the lens design on the booth walls . . . I don't know."

Perhaps it was Kara's frown that put Jason off and made him cut his idea short. She liked it, but she was just assessing the implications of having Michel work for her again. She had been looking forward to having a relationship with him without In-A-Wink involved.

She dismissed her staff and, as they left her office, she folded the corner of the page in the magazine. There would be time enough for gadgets on Monday. She sat at her desk looking out the window. When everybody had gone home, and she could hear the whir of the vacuum in the outside offices, she picked up the phone and dialed Michel's number.

* * *

Saturday dawned warm and sunny. Kara took her breakfast and newspaper out to the deck and watched the dew steam off the garden. She had brought the European magazine home with her, but it was still tucked away in her briefcase. No matter how exciting her find, she knew that she would get no work done today.

Maybe I'll show it to Michel tonight, she thought, *and get his reaction.*

She skimmed the newspaper, not really interested in the growing crime rate and falling economy. Her mind was far away, in a gazebo on a hill beside a river.

The phone rang, a double, long-distance ring.

"Hello?"

"There you are!" Monica sounded cross.

"Hello, Mother." Kara kept the disappointment from her voice. Last night she had left a message for Michel, an invitation to dinner and a proposal for him to design their Photokina booth. She had not yet heard back from him.

"And just where have you been?" asked Monica, as if Kara was still a teenager. "I've been calling all week and there was no answer." Kara didn't bother to ask why Monica didn't leave a message. Her mother did not trust answering machines. Kara suspected that she feared saying the wrong thing and having it captured on tape.

"I was out, Mom. I didn't realize that I had to check in with you." As soon as Kara said it, she knew she had just picked a fight, but she was tired of hedging around her mother's moods.

"Don't get smart with me," said Monica. "I was worried, that's all." Warning bells went off in Kara's head. Monica's pettishness heralded the first signs of depression. Over the years, Kara had gone through so many ups and downs with her mother that she had learned to read the signs. She changed her tone immediately.

"I had a date, Mom."

That ought to cheer her up, she thought, but Monica was not appeased.

"With who?"

"A nice man, a painter. We went out for dinner." She didn't mention Matthew or the gazebo.

"What is he? One of those students that paints houses?"

"Not houses, Mom, paintings."

"Great, a starving artist. He's probably after you for your money." Kara tried not to laugh. In-A-Wink had made her comfortably well off, but she was by no means rich, certainly not by Michel's Senneville standards.

"So you can support him while he paints nudes."

This time Kara did laugh.

"Oh, Mom! You're so old-fashioned. He doesn't paint nudes. He paints nature scenes, and he's far from starving. He has a house in Senneville."

"Hmph," snorted Monica. For the time being, she had nothing else to criticize. "So you haven't heard from Matthew, then?"

Kara wanted to scream. Did Monica really think that if Matthew called she would go running to him? In her mother's world women didn't break engagements or fire men. Kara took a deep breath and willed herself not to be baited.

"No, I haven't heard from Matthew. I hear that he is very busy with his new job."

That's an understatement, she thought. They chatted a bit more about nothing in particular.

"What's his name?" asked Monica, before hanging up. For a moment, Kara had difficulty following the trail of her mother's thoughts, another sure sign that she was headed for depression. "The painter," prompted Monica. "What's his name?"

"Oh. Michel," said Kara. "Michel Vernier. You might have heard about him. His latest show was quite a success."

"Hmph," was Monica's only response.

Kara made a mental note to call her mother tomorrow, and the next day. When Monica edged toward depression it was better to bear the brunt of her moods day to day rather than let them build up over the week until paranoia ruled her emotions.

In the past, Monica had called Kara after only a few days and harangued her for being a rotten daughter and for abandoning her mother. Once she accused Kara of despising her since childhood, and that, being a selfless mother, she had ignored Kara's feelings to take care of her. The conversation only deteriorated from there, so that when Kara hung up, she immediately dialed Monica's doctor.

''There's nothing I can do, Kara,'' said Dr. Hanson. ''Your mother won't see a specialist and I don't want to give her anything stronger without knowing exactly what we're dealing with.'' But Dr. Hanson was a kind man and he stopped by Monica's house for coffee and surreptitiously verified that she still took her medication.

Perhaps Monica only needed some attention because her mood brightened after the doctor's visit. Kara's mood darkened, though. Was she supposed to provide that attention? Was a child responsible for a parent's mental health? She resented the drain on her emotions and felt guilty for that. Monica was not a problem that would go away. Kara just wished that she could assert herself with her mother, that she could mount an offense instead of always shrinking away and leaving the encounter with feelings of guilt and inadequacy.

Kara had been thinking about all this with the phone still cradled in her hand. The receiver started to beep in her hand and she hung it up. She decided to wait another few days before calling Dr. Hanson.

The phone rang again immediately. Michel greeted her with a friendly hello. He said that he would love to design the booth but he was too busy for dinner. Kara was relieved and disappointed in the same heartbeat.

''How about tomorrow afternoon?'' he asked.

''Sure,'' said Kara. ''I could come down to your studio if you're busy.''

"No, that's all right. I've some errands to run in town. How about the old port again?

"Fine by me."

They made arrangements to meet at four o'clock.

So he still won't let me see his studio, thought Kara. *What a strange bird.*

She called Annie and invited her over for a spaghetti dinner and then changed into her garden clothes. A day in the fresh air would do her good.

"A lenstick?" asked Annie. They had cleared away the supper dishes and Kara had placed the French magazine on the table in front of them.

"Yeah. Get it?" Kara fidgeted in her seat. It was clear that she was excited by this prospect. "Because it's no bigger than a lipstick, but it cleans cameras. See?" She pointed at another picture. "That end has a pop-out brush and the other is for cleaning fingerprints. Some new powder that eliminates the need for cleaning liquid, I gather. And look, those little feet pop out and turn it into a mini-tripod. Clever, eh?"

"Ingenious," said Annie. "Let's hope it works." She knew as well as Kara that a good gadget was the retailer's bread and butter. They made little profit on hardware and films, but a hot accessory—especially one small enough to stock beside the cash register—was the sort of thing that kept them in business. An exclusive distributor could make the year with such an item.

"It could sell for under twenty dollars, I think," said Kara.

"Not much under twenty, though. You don't want people thinking it's cheap. This is the gadget they *must* have." Kara was reminded again why she valued Annie's input. She articulated Kara's thoughts so that she understood them better.

"Okay," said Annie, closing the magazine. "I agree. It's a hot item. Now enough about business. I've been waiting patiently all week. Tell me about your painter."

My painter, thought Kara. *I wish.*

She described the details of their evening together, glossing over the romantic encounter in the gazebo, but Annie demanded details of her clash with Matthew.

"Brenda Rosen?" asked Annie, shaking her head. "Are you sure it was her?"

"Uh-huh."

"That's not good."

"No. I was counting on her usual order to make our numbers this month."

"Actually," said Annie, pulling out her appointment book, "If I'm not mistaken . . ." She flipped through some pages. "Yes, here it is. She's already placed an order."

"Well, then she's planning her Christmas bump. If we lose the Rosen account, there will be layoffs before December."

The two women sipped their coffee in silence.

"Don't panic yet," said Annie. "Matthew has been known to let his charm slip."

Kara snorted.

"Just make sure the boys in sales pay extra attention to the Rosens."

"Mmm. Maybe you should call her yourself, Kara."

"I will, but not before I get the deal for this lenstick. I want to personally introduce it."

They sat quietly again, each worrying about the coming season, each making mental notes of people to call, prices to check, promotions to put in gear.

Kara refilled their cups from the carafe on the coffee warmer.

"One more thing," said Kara. "I want you to check around. Call in some favors and find out what Matthew is up to. He's been visiting my mother."

"Your mother?" Annie's eyebrows shot up to her hairline. "You're kidding?" Kara shook her head. "He is up to something. I'll make some calls Monday. We'll do everything Monday. Just like we always do. In the meantime, don't tell me that Matthew was the highlight of your evening. That gazebo sounded awfully romantic."

Kara laughed.

"It was romantic. *He* is romantic." Kara wouldn't say his name. Just hearing it in her head—Michel, with the soft *ch* like his breath on her neck—made her stomach tighten, but to say it out loud, to feel it on her tongue, that was something she wished to reserve for when they were alone together.

"Actually," she said, pulling her thoughts back from her musing, "he reminds me of you."

"Me?" laughed Annie. "You mean old and worn?"

"No! I mean that he always seems to know what I'm thinking."

"Well, you are a bit of an open book, my dear. When you're happy, your eyes glow. When you're angry that funny red line appears on your nose."

"Red line!" cried Kara.

"And"—Annie held up her hand to ward off Kara's protests—"when you're worried, you chew your bottom lip."

"Am I really that bad?" laughed Kara.

"Uh-huh."

"So why couldn't Matthew ever read me?"

"You can't compare Michel with Matthew. Michel is an *artiste*," she gave the word a heavy French drawl, "an observer. Matthew is egocentric. He can't see past the end of his nose."

"Well, thank goodness, it's a big one then," said Kara, and the two women collapsed into giggles. The remainder of the evening deteriorated into a critique of all the noses in the office.

Chapter Seven

In her suite at the hotel in Cologne, Kara unpacked her clothes, and hung them in the closet. She would be there for ten days and now wished that she had brought fewer businesslike outfits. Her shoes had been chosen for comfort—she would be manning the booth all day—and her eveningwear for business. Now that Michel had joined their team, she cursed herself for not including at least one little black dress.

After their meeting at the old port in Montreal six weeks ago, Michel had agreed to design and set up the booth in Germany. Kara was glad that they had kept the meeting short. Though he was obviously preoccupied with his coming show, Michel had been friendly and amusing. Several times Kara had re-sisted the urge to touch him. It seeded so natural to want to do so, and yet she enjoyed their new amia-ble, but charged relationship. It wouldn't take much, though, to push them over the edge to full-blown romance.

Michel, too, was holding back. He spoke of his work and was clearly anxious to get back to his studio.

She had not seen him in the intervening weeks, but Kara was grateful that he had given up his precious time to help them. He was leaving Cologne for New York on Tuesday, two short days away, for the opening of his new show. Kara wished that she could be there for his debut. She had not even seen his new paintings, though on the flight over, he had described them to her. She loved to listen to his voice when he spoke of his work. He had held her hand, nervously rubbing her fingers over and over. He was usually so self-assured; Kara found it endearing that he could be shy about his work. She felt honored that he would let her into his world in this way.

They worked well as a team. The design and production of the booth had gone off without a hitch. Michel had recreated the artwork from the Prolar packaging on several eight-foot plywood sheets. The yellow backdrops would make them stand out among the thousands of other booths and, they hoped, generate the media attention that they needed. Jason, who had been in Germany already for two days, had suggested that they give away lensticks to the first thousand customers to come by, a bit expensive of a giveaway, but Kara had agreed. They needed to get them into the marketplace so that people would start asking for them.

She called down to the reception to see if the boxes of lensticks had arrived and was assured that they were waiting for her at reception. As she hung up the phone, there was a knock at her door. Both Michel and Jason stood in the hallway, dressed casually in jeans and sweaters.

"We're going down for a bite," said Jason. "Are you coming?"

Kara glanced back at her messy room. Her clothes were still not unpacked. The desk was lost under stacks of papers. Boxes of displays were piled haphazardly against one wall.

"All right," she said, closing the door on the disarray. "But no carousing. We've got quite a day tomorrow. That booth is more difficult to put together than you guys think."

Jason cocked his head to one side and pouted.

"Aw, come on boss. I can't leave without sampling the famous Kölsch beer." Kara laughed, pushing the two of them ahead of her down the hall. As the elevator doors closed, she leaned against the wall and closed her eyes. She was already tired, and the week hadn't even started yet. Michel rubbed her shoulder absently. Kara liked the unaffected gesture. It was comfortable, something a friend would do to another friend, or a husband to his wife.

When the elevator doors opened in the lobby, they came face to face with Matthew. For several seconds the In-A-Wink team stared at him. As the elevator doors began to close again, Matthew stuck his foot inside.

"Hello, Matthew," said Jason, breaking the silence.

"Jason." Matthew inclined his head. "Kara." He pointedly ignored Michel.

"You're not staying here, too?" asked Kara, not bothering to hide her disappointment.

"Wouldn't dream of it. I'm just here to meet a friend. My hotel is beside the exhibition center."

Kara ignored the implied slight. Photokina was held at the enormous KölnMesse, forty-five minutes away from their hotel. Even if she could have found rooms near the Messe, In-A-Wink could never have budgeted for that expense.

Jason and Matthew exchanged brief pleasantries, but Kara pushed past them and walked straight-backed through the lobby to the pub-style restaurant near the front of the hotel. Michel and Matthew joined her in the booth moments later. Kara was grateful to feel Michel's hand grip hers under the table.

"He's up to something," said Kara, after the waitress had left with their orders.

"Nonsense," said Michel. "You're just stressed from the trip."

"He's only visiting," assured Jason. "A coincidence, that's all. You shouldn't let him get to you."

"Oh, Kara can hold her own," said Michel. "You should have heard the lambasting she gave Mr. Richmond last time we met in Montreal." Michel recounted the exchange from the Claremont Cafe. "Her words were so caustic, it was as if she had thrown acid in his face!"

Kara tried not to be embarrassed by the teasing

praise. She said nothing else on the subject. In her heart she knew that Matthew's appearance in their hotel, out of thousands in the city, was no coincidence. Annie's inquiries into Matthew's schemes had turned up nothing. Nonetheless, Kara was certain that Matthew was still plotting his revenge.

Jason and Michel bantered on about the medieval costumes of the waitresses, but Kara hardly heard them. "Did you check the booth," she interrupted. "Did it arrive in one piece?"

"Everything's there," said Michel. "I'll have only a few touchups to do tomorrow after it's set up."

"And the giveaways?" she asked Jason. "I called down to see if they had arrived, but I didn't actually go see."

"Relax, Boss," Jason said with a smile. "I checked."

"I'm worried we're not going to have enough time to set up." She pulled her appointment book out of her purse and flipped through several pages. The men fell silent and she could feel their eyes on her. She looked up. Jason was smiling at her, but Michel's brow was creased in a frown. He covered her hand in his and closed the appointment book.

"Tomorrow, Kara," he said. "Tomorrow we will have time to worry about everything."

Kara smiled tensely. She took another long draught of beer and tried to put aside her anxiety. Tomorrow they would find out what Matthew was up to. She only hoped that he had channeled his anger into something positive like his own Photokina presentation. A good dose of competition might even highlight In-A-Wink's creative efforts, but somehow, she suspected that Matthew's intentions were more sinister.

Back in her room after dinner, Kara sat in a plush chair and looked out at the cityscape. Over several rooftops she could see the lighted towers of Cologne's famous Dom, a gothic cathedral whose history stretched back to the Middle Ages. She wished that they would have the time to go explore it, but the busy schedule of Photokina left little room for sightseeing.

She relaxed her body into the comfortable chair and wished that her mind could follow suit. She needed sleep, but her head buzzed with worries and ideas. She sighed and opened her appointment book again. There would be no resting tonight.

A few moments later, Michel knocked on her door. She answered distractedly, expecting the chambermaid.

"Do you ever put that book down?" asked Michel, standing over her. Kara dropped the book to her desk, but still clutched its leather binding so that she didn't reach out for him. Unconsciously, she had been waiting for him. As he stood in front of her desk, lit from behind, he looked like an angel come to rescue her from herself. His stubbly beard accentuated his dark eyes. Separated by four feet, they stared at each other, letting their eyes speak words that neither of them dared to utter.

"Want to take a walk?" asked Michel. His voice was thick, as if he had just woken from an unsettling dream.

Not trusting her own voice, Kara nodded and grabbed a sweater on her way out. Once in the cool evening air, safely away from the privacy of her room, Michel laced Kara's fingers in his own and tucked both their hands into his jacket pocket. Instinctively, they headed toward the lights of the Dom.

From somewhere inside his jacket, Michel produced a tourist guide. As the majestic slate-gray towers of the Dom rose before them, he recited its history.

"Six hundred years to build . . . fourteen bombs hit it during World War II . . . says here that the tower holds the world's heaviest bell . . ."

Kara enjoyed the sound of his voice, his closeness, the feel of his fingers wrapped around her own. She marveled at how intimate she could feel with this man, a man whom she had seen only half a dozen times in her life.

They stood for several minutes in the square before the Dom, taking in the bustling activity. Young people sat on the stairs that led to the cathedral. Mimes and caricaturists displayed their talents to the many tourists that mingled in the square. The sun still glowed faintly in the western sky, but was outshone by the lighted towers. They sat on a stone bench and gazed up at their splendor.

"Do you know that I feel very close to you," said Kara, leaning back on Michel.

"I should hope so. You're sitting on my hand." She jumped up as if she had been bitten by a spider.

"Just kidding," he said, laughing. "Come back here." He pulled her back down on the bench, this time sitting her between his legs and wrapping his arms tightly around her.

"I know exactly what you mean," he said quietly, nuzzling her neck. "I feel very close to you, too." She relaxed against him and they watched the mimes and jugglers for several minutes. Within the warmth of his embrace, the tensions of the day ebbed from her muscles.

"It's about time that you relaxed," he said, feeling her slump against him.

"I know," said Kara, "It's just that so much is riding on this show, you have no idea, and Matthew," she almost spit the name out. "I'm sure that was not a coincidence. He's up to something."

"Mmm. I'd like to say that you're being paranoid, but I get that same feeling."

"I just hope that we can take what ever he throws at us."

Michel laughed.

"If anyone can handle that weasel, it's you, Kara S. Mackenzie. He doesn't stand a chance."

"Maybe he's spying. Maybe he's already seen our booth and is planning to outdo us. Maybe he's discovered the lensticks. Do you think he could get the contract away from us? It's not signed yet . . ."

"Kara, relax!" Michel squeezed her shoulders. "Listen to yourself. Brooks don't babble as much as you. Matthew and his schemes can't hurt you. Your product is secure for one night, and your booth will be fabulous. I promise."

"I didn't mean to imply that your work is not good, Michel." She twisted in her seat to look at him. He was so close she could have kissed him. "I know that the booth will turn some heads, but we may need more than that. I haven't told anybody yet, but In-A-Wink is in serious financial trouble. If we don't win back some accounts at this show I'll have to lay off staff before Christmas."

Michel was quiet for several seconds. Clearly, he had not guessed at the gravity of the situation. Kara wondered if she had said too much, and yet Michel always made her feel that she could tell him anything. And then, when he finally spoke, Kara knew that she was in love with this man. He didn't comment on her business sense. He didn't try to console her. He didn't belittle her situation. Instead, he zeroed in on the one thing that truly worried her: the staff.

"You are not responsible for other people's lives, Kara. You do your best, you treat them well, and if it doesn't work out, they'll find other employment. You've got a great bunch of people working for you, they'll understand."

Kara put her arms around him and buried her face

under his chin. It was so good to have a friend, someone who understood her. Michel lifted her chin and looked into her eyes.

"I'm not crying," she said, with a slight sniffle.

"Just checking." He smiled and kissed the tip of her cold nose. He kissed her damp eyes and the corner of her mouth. Kara turned into him and their lips met with an urgency she had never felt before. He pulled away first and held her face cupped between both his hands. He touched her cheeks, her ears, her eyebrows. He traced the line of her mouth with the tip of one finger.

I love you, she thought, not daring to say it out loud, but content to know it herself.

He kissed her again, gently, and then he turned her around so that she leaned against him again. Without words, the gesture said: not yet.

Kara sighed to herself, content to wait. Soon Photokina would be over. Michel would go to New York and come back a success, and then . . . And then what? She dared not think about it now. It was enough to share this moment with him, beside a beautiful cathedral in a beautiful city.

Kara came down for breakfast the next morning dressed in jeans and a sweatshirt. They had just one day to set up their booth at the KölnMesse, and it would be a long one. She wore her hair pulled out of the way and little makeup, but her complexion was radiant, as if suffused with a glow of happiness. All her warm feelings disappeared, however, when

she saw Jason waiting for her in the lobby. His dark expression told her that something was terribly wrong.

"Someone broke into the storage area last night," he said.

"The booth?" asked Kara, though she already knew the answer.

"It's, uh, been damaged."

Kara's heart sank.

"How bad?"

"Bad," said Jason. "The concierge won't admit it, but I'm sure this was an inside job. The boards were painted over in black. All of them. Whoever did this had hours to work undisturbed."

All Michel's beautiful work! thought Kara with a pang of sorrow. She had hoped to mount the tableaux in the office after the show, and now they were erased.

"Oh, no!" Her regret instantly changed to alarm. "What are we going to do? We have no booth and the show starts in less than twenty-four hours!"

"I don't know," said Jason, "but Michel seems to. He told me to go buy some more paint and said he'd meet us at the Messe in two hours."

"He can't possibly think to redo them? They took weeks to paint."

Matthew had done this. Had their things been stolen or simply ransacked, there might have been some doubt, but this calculated sabotage was the work of a vindictive mind. The audacity of the crime insulted

her. Matthew wanted Kara to know that he was responsible for her ruin.

"What about the sample lensticks?" she asked suddenly.

"They're safe," said Jason, with a shy smile. "I had them brought up to my room last night. I guess your anxiety wore off on me."

"Thank goodness for small miracles," said Kara. "Let's go get some breakfast before I beat the concierge about the head with a stick."

After half an hour of threats and curses, the hotel manager finally agreed to compensate Kara to her satisfaction. They still had no booth for the most important trade show of the year, but at least she had forced them to take responsibility for their transgression.

They had rented a van to transport all their supplies to the Messe. During the forty-five-minute drive, Kara stared out the window at the gray clouds, the gray pavement, and the gray water that passed under the gray bridge. Her victory over the hotel management seemed minor now. She had failed in another, bigger way. After coming so close to turning her fortune around, they would never be able to generate enough media interest in their products now, not with a plain black booth. By the time they reached the exhibition hall, Kara was already deciding whom to lay off first.

When they arrived at the Messe, Jason began setting up the eight-by-eight sheets of plywood, now painted solid black, that would make up the booth.

Michel sighed when he saw the damage, but immediately began painting over the first panel. Kara realised how distressing it must be for him, to see his weeks of hard work vanish in one night.

"I'm sorry," she said, reaching out to him. He was crouched near the floor, painting in the backdrop, but he smiled and took her hand.

"You're ex-fiancé is my toughest critic yet," he said. "I've had my work dismissed, maligned, and ridiculed, but never erased."

"I wish I could prove it was him," said Kara, though she didn't know what she would do with that proof. The hall was filling up with businesspeople setting up their own booths. Kara scanned the large room looking for Matthew.

"Let it go, Kara," said Michel. His hair tumbled over his forehead in a mess. He brushed it away, and continued painting. "He's had his fun. Now he'll probably leave us alone. I'm going to redo the panels, though I won't have time to re-create the Prolar packages." He shrugged. "So I'll do something else, and who knows, maybe it will be better." Kara appreciated his effort, but she doubted his words. He tugged on her pant leg, forcing her to look at him.

"I promised you that your booth would be sensational, and so it will be."

Kara opened her mouth to protest but Michel cut her off.

"Kara, trust me, okay?" He looked so beseeching, down on one knee as if he were proposing marriage.

Mutely, she nodded. What other choice did she have?

"Why don't you go help Jason put up the rest of the panels," suggested Michel, "before he gets a hernia."

When they were all set up, Kara went to get coffee and muffins for everyone and then Michel put them all to work. Jason painted one whole panel pink while Kara split another in two and painted the top half blue and the bottom green.

"I'm not very good at this," she said with a critical eye. It wasn't as easy as she would have thought just to paint one solid color without streaking.

"Don't worry," said Michel. "You're just doing the background. I'm going to go over it all anyway. I'm just impressed that you haven't spilled any paint yet." He winked at her.

"Very funny. There." She painted a large green spot on the end of his nose. "What do you think of my artwork now?"

"Oh, Madame," said Michel, waving his red paintbrush at her dauntingly. "I strongly suggest you don't start a paint war with me, because I will surely win."

"All right." She reached out and wiped the paint off his face with a rag. "Wait, there's more." He stood still and let her clean him, all the while never taking his eyes from her.

He wants to kiss me, she thought. *I can see it in his eyes.* Her hand shook slightly as she wiped the last of the paint from his face.

"We'll never finish in time if you two don't stop playing games," said Jason.

He's right, thought Kara, with a pang of guilt. Here she was having fun when the fate of In-A-Wink hung in the balance. Fairly chastised, she worked diligently through the morning and afternoon, stopping only once for sandwiches. She called Annie to fill her in on this new disaster and to keep tabs on the office. "Don't let him get away with this, Kara," Annie warned.

The organizers of Photokina had been sympathetic to their plight and had provided a heavy curtain to pull around their section while they worked. So while they could hear all the bustle going on in the enormous hall, they were left alone. Kara fully expected Matthew to come by to inspect his handiwork.

By late afternoon, Michel had finished two panels. One resembled an antique parlor with gilded mirrors and Victorian settees. The other seemed like an adjoining dining room set for a Christmas feast.

"I still don't know what you're up to," said Kara, surveying his handiwork, "but I like it."

Michel just smiled at her. For the past several hours he had been in deep concentration, barely aware of the noise from the exhibition hall or of Kara and Jason. Kara was reminded of the first time she met him, when he painted the mural in their office building. She wondered if his focused devotion to his work would bother her one day. Just as quickly as these thoughts entered her mind, she banished them. Already she was thinking like a jealous wife and they'd really only been on one date!

She looked at her watch. It was nearly five o'clock. She felt guilty about leaving Michel to finish the booth, knowing that he would probably be there most of the night, but she had an important dinner date set up, and now, more than ever, she needed to network the right people and bring in the orders.

"Don't worry about me," said Michel, standing up, and stretching out his broad shoulders. "This is the most fun I've had in a long time. I'll get it done tonight. I'm running on adrenaline now."

Jason agreed to stay and keep Michel company and make sure he ate dinner. He also would make arrangements with the Messe security to have a guard posted at their booth all night. Kara deemed this a worthwhile expense. She didn't want to wake up tomorrow and find another black booth.

As she parted the curtains to leave, Kara spotted Matthew across the hall, standing with a group of his associates. He held a cocktail glass in one hand and when he saw her, he shook the ice cubes in his glass and raised it in a toast.

All day, as she painted backdrops, she had planned her inevitable confrontation with Matthew. She had considered her words carefully, but now when she saw his smirking grin, she almost lost it. She wanted to pitch that cocktail in his face. Her feet moved with their own volition and she crossed the expanse of the hall in seconds.

"Kara!" said Matthew with faked enthusiasm. "How lovely to see you."

Kara grabbed his glass from his hand, but instead of emptying it on his head, she downed it in one gulp.

"Thank you," she said, handing him the empty glass. "Parched throat."

"Anything for an old friend."

Matthew's acquaintances watched the exchange with barely suppressed curiosity. Everyone in the industry knew of their volatile past, and Kara suspected that a few of these men also knew about Matthew's midnight escapade.

"How's the booth coming along?" asked Matthew with pretended innocence. "All that secrecy with the curtains. We thought you might be building Frankenstein in there."

"No, no," laughed Kara. "We just wanted to pretty up the place a bit. We're hoping to make a big splash tomorrow, though I see that we have some stiff competition." She glanced around at their booth. Pamphlets were laid out neatly on one table. Blue curtains were hung behind with logos from their different lines. Kara almost smirked when she saw a pyramid of empty demo boxes piled in one corner—plain blue boxes with respectable black lettering.

About as stiff as a stick in the mud, she thought, feeling a surge of excitement. Their original plans may have been foiled, but she knew that with a creative genius like Michel in her corner, she could still beat these old humdrums.

She chatted a few minutes with Matthew's boss, a man who had been in the industry as long as she, and a rival whom she respected, before making her excuses.

"Good luck tomorrow," she said. "I must run, though. I'm having dinner with Brenda Rosen." Out of the corner of one eye she saw Matthew's startled look when she mentioned the name.

So, thought Kara, *he thinks he's got that account all sewn up. We'll see about that.*

In the taxi, she took out her beloved appointment book and planned her attack. Booth or no booth, she would win back the Rosen account tonight.

As it turned out, Kara hadn't needed all her careful planning. She arrived at the restaurant bearing the gift of a lenstick. Brenda immediately saw the potential of such a product. She promised to place a huge order, but refused to talk business that night.

"I'll be the first one at your booth tomorrow," said Brenda, lighting a cigarette, "but tonight I just wanted some friendly company and"—she paused here, put her cigarette down and took a sip of water—"I don't normally get involved in the squabbles between my suppliers. You've always worked so hard for me, Kara, and though business demands that I buy from many suppliers, I always felt a special bond for you. I think you should know that Matthew is planning something drastic."

Kara nodded.

"I know." She told Brenda about the booth and her suspicions.

"That's dirty," said Brenda. "Have you spoken to him today?" Kara described their meeting, and Brenda grinned.

"You handled that with class, Kara. I think it's time that Mr. Richmond was knocked down a peg or two. I'm going to start a rumor that he tried to sabotage your booth."

"That's not a rumor," said Kara. "That's the truth."

"Yes," smiled Brenda viciously. "That's the beauty of it. All good rumors star with a grain of truth, but who knows where it could lead. By the time it snowballs through the old boys' network, Matthew could be a convicted felon."

Kara laughed at her wickedness. She might have once been shocked at her own feelings of vindictiveness, but Matthew had struck her where it hurts, and she no longer cared what happened to him. His actions were no longer her responsibility. With a sense of relief, Kara knew that she was truly over Matthew Richmond, which was perhaps the best revenge of all.

The two women spent the rest of the evening conspiring against Matthew. The plots became more extravagant. Kara knew that she would never carry any of them out, but it was great fun anyway.

Kara was tired as she rode the elevator up to her room. She wondered if Michel had finished the booth, if he was in his room, just beside her own. She thought about knocking on his door, but it was late and she knew that he would be tired too.

She fumbled with the lock on her door, swearing softly when she dropped her purse with a clang of keys and cosmetics. She finally opened the door and searched in the dark for the light switch as the phone rang.

"You're home late," said Michel without a hello. He sounded tired and angry.

"Yes, I guess I am," answered Kara, confused by his tone.

"Did you schmooze well? Make any big sales?"

"Um, yes and no." Why was he so angry? Because she had gone out without him? Because she was so late? Her head spun and her thoughts were not clear. She told him that she was tired and hung up the phone.

Five minutes later there was a knock on her door. Michel stood in the hallway, dressed in cotton sweats and a T-shirt, bearing two cups of steaming hot chocolate.

"Sorry about the second degree," he said, handing her a cup. "I guess I was just worried. You were out so late in a strange city."

"I'm a big girl, Michel. I can take care of myself." What right did he have to keep tabs on her? She put the cup of chocolate down without tasting it.

Michel looked at her for several minutes. He reached out for her, but she moved away, and pretended to be interested in the movie reviews that were mounted on the TV. Finally, he set his own cup down and said, "You're right, you can take care of yourself." And then he turn and left.

Kara went through her bedtime rituals by rote, trying to ignore the empty feeling inside her. By the time she fell asleep, the cups of chocolate were stone cold.

She woke before daylight when a waiter knocked on her door with breakfast.

"Compliments of the monsieur next door," said the waiter.

Kara smiled. Already their harsh words seemed far away. She noticed that the breakfast tray was set for two, and rushed to wash the sleep from her face before Michel appeared at her door.

She pushed aside the papers that covered the breakfast table and laid out the tray just as he knocked.

"I'm sorry," was the first thing he said, taking her in his arms.

"Me too," answered Kara. He was freshly showered and Kara breathed in his clean scent. "I think I was exhausted."

"Mmm, I could tell," said Michel, pulling away. He sat at the table and poured the coffee. "Did you have a good time?" His voice was still hesitant. He was clearly bothered still, but didn't want to turn it into another argument.

Did he think that she had been out carousing all

night while he worked? Or that she had spent the evening with someone else? She wondered if she should ask him, but he offered the insight himself.

"It's been a long time since I felt jealousy, Kara. I think it took me by surprise." He did not reach out to touch her, but his words seemed like a caress.

"I didn't know that you were the kind to get jealous," she said. Part of her wanted to let him believe that she had been out with a man, to see where his jealousy would lead them, but something told her that Michel was not a man to be trifled with.

"There are many things that you don't know about me, Kara."

And so many that I want to learn, she thought.

"Do you remember when you felt out of your element at the gallery?" he asked. Kara nodded. "In a way, that's how I feel when I think of you with all those businessmen, talking shop, making contacts. It's a world that I could never fit into."

Kara thought of her own jealousy toward the reporter at the gallery, a jealousy that had been born of her sense of alienation among all the art critics and patrons.

"Do you remember that woman who was with Matthew at Claremont Cafe?" Kara asked. Michel nodded. "I was out with her last night."

Michel didn't say anything, but he had the grace to look sheepish.

"She wanted to warn me that Matthew was up to no good."

"No kidding," Michel said as he spread jam over

a piece of toast. "Here." He handed it to Kara. "Come sit down. You've a long day ahead, and you need fortification."

Kara accepted the toast. Michel tucked a napkin in the front of her robe, making Kara aware that he could touch her if he wanted to. He poured cream into her coffee.

"Sugar?"

Kara nodded. It was nice to be fussed over.

"Did you finish last night?" she asked.

"Uh-huh. You know, Matthew might rue the day he wrecked your booth. I think the new one is even more spectacular than the old." Kara must have looked doubtful, because he added sternly: "I promised you, Kara, that your booth would be spectacular. I mean to keep that promise. I do have a reputation to uphold after all." He smiled at her and suddenly the KölnMesse seemed very far away. She almost wished that the opening of Photokina was not today, that they had more time to explore the city and see the sights together, but Michel was leaving for New York in the morning.

Kara put down her coffee cup. She circled the small breakfast table and took Michel's cup from him too. He grinned at her as she sat herself on his lap.

"Know what?" she asked, circling her arms around his neck.

"Hmm?" He closed his eyes and let her trace the line around his eyes and mouth, just as she had so often wanted to.

"I'm glad you're not one of those stuffy old businessmen."

Michel opened his eyes and smiled at her. For the next half hour of breakfast, Photokina and business were all forgotten.

When they arrived at the Messe the mimes were waiting for them.

"Don't call them mimes," warned Michel, grinning at her astonishment. "They're performance artists."

"Where did you find them?" asked Kara. Michel shrugged.

"Artists find artists."

They were an Abbot and Costello sort of pair. Arthur was tall and thin with a mane of alarmingly red hair. He had long arms and long hands with fingers that were able to contort into any shape, so that even though he didn't speak, his intentions were always clear.

Clyde, standing on his tiptoes, did not reach Arthur's shoulder. He was fair with dark hair and was dressed, like Arthur, as the perfect Edwardian gentleman. Kara understood their purpose when she saw the pair against Michel's painted backdrops. Each panel, depicted some part of an old English country house: the parlor, the gaming room, the garden (with a suspiciously familiar gazebo), and the dining hall. Antique chairs were placed on the side of the parlor for clients to sit in, as was a wrought iron bench near the gardens. The effect was astonishingly realistic.

Arthur sat Kara down in one of the chairs, while Clyde poured her a coffee from an ornate urn.

"I feel like Jane Eyre!" laughed Kara. Clyde nodded his head vigorously.

Just then, Jason appeared with a box of lensticks.

"The rest are in the holding area," he said, "but this ought to do for now." He handed a dozen to each of the mimes and set the rest on a display table.

"Well," said Kara, "let's get started."

Within half an hour, they had products arrayed over every available surface in the booth. Kara noted with pride how vivid the Prolar lens boxes were, especially when compared with the competition's.

By midafternoon they had already given out hundreds of lensticks. Arthur and Clyde were a sensational hit. They simply went out into the crowd and pulled in unsuspecting customers. Their bungling charm won people over before they even realized that they were being solicited. Clyde had, slung around his neck and shoulders, a dizzying array of cameras, all with Prolar lenses attached. Without words, they pretended to be confused tourists and stopped people to have their pictures taken in the garden or the parlor. Almost everybody accepted with grace, and Kara was pleased that so many people were able to handle the lenses. They generated more than enough interest to keep Kara and Jason busy for the morning.

"Can you take those films over to one of the photo finishing booths?" Kara asked Michel. "We'll tell everyone to come back later for their pictures with the red-haired giant.'' Kara could see that they were causing a stir. People at other booths pointed at them, and, as the day progressed, the traffic to their own booth increased exponentially.

During a brief lull in the afternoon, Kara sent Jason to buy them all coffee and sandwiches. None of them had had time for lunch.

''Thank you,'' Kara said to Michel, as they sat side by side on the wrought-iron bench in his painted garden. She wanted to say so much more, to tell him how grateful she was that he understood her vision for the future of In-A-Wink. He had created a living work of art that reflected everything she found inspiring and fun about photography. She now knew that together, given the chance, they could revolutionize markets of art and photography. She wanted to tell him all that and also beg him not to go to New York tomorrow, but she knew that was unfair.

''It was my pleasure,'' said Michel. ''I enjoyed the challenge. It gave me time to think about something but my own work. Artists can be a little selfish, you know.''

Kara immediately felt guilty about monopolizing his time. She began plotting ways in which to make it up to him, but by the time Jason returned with their sandwiches, there was already a crowd around the table again, and the next time she had to think about it was well after eight o'clock, Michel pulled her aside to say that he was heading back to the hotel.

"I'm exhausted," he said, "and I've got an early flight tomorrow."

"Of course," Kara said quickly. She didn't really want him to go. She had come to enjoy the feeling of having him beside her all day, but he did look haggard. His normally sparkling eyes were flat and his complexion a pale gray. "I didn't expect you to stay even so long."

He squeezed her hand and kissed her gently on the cheek, but there was no time for more as another crowd of potential clients was impatiently waiting for her attention. She watched him walk across the hall even as she spoke to the young man in front of her. As Michel left the Messe, he turned back to look at her and she smiled. Just then, she caught Matthew's eye. His booth was strategically placed near the entrance. He must have seen the exchange between Kara and Michel, because he scowled. Kara almost laughed to herself. How pathetic he seemed now! She had seen a steady stream of people file past his booth, but nothing compared to the action that Arthur and Clyde had produced for In-A-Wink. But Kara no longer wished Matthew ill. In fact, she wished him success, if only marginally, but enough so that his vindictive nature did not seek vengeance on In-A-Wink again.

The show closed at nine o'clock. By the time they had packed everything up it was closer to ten, and then of course began the schmooze-fest. Every year at Photokina it was the same thing: the real negotiations began only after the hall closed for the night.

The many lounges in and around the Messe were filled with people from the industry.

Kara thought about letting Jason go at it alone, and slipping back to the hotel to spend the last evening with Michel, but Clyde and Arthur apparently wanted their day's wages in beer and the three of them coaxed her into just one drink at the nearest lounge. The place was buzzing with excitement as was usual for the opening day. Clyde and Arthur continued to make a stir and Kara wondered where they got their energy.

By eleven-thirty she could barely keep her eyes open.

"Give them anything they want," Kara said to Jason, inclining her head to their dynamic duo, "within reason. And remind them that they have another full day tomorrow."

"Aye, aye, captain," said Jason. "But don't worry. I have a feeling that this is a normal day for them."

Jason, too, looked tired, and Kara was glad that her other two salesmen would arrive in Cologne tomorrow to take some of the pressure off.

It was after midnight when she reached her room. She listened outside Michel's door for several seconds, but could hear nothing. She didn't want to wake him but decided to set her alarm for five in the morning so that she could say goodbye. After her head hit the pillow, she didn't remember another thing until morning when she was awakened by a loud banging on her door.

She stumbled out of bed and threw on her robe. It was after eight o'clock.

Michel!

But it was Jason who stood in the doorway. Michel was already halfway to New York.

"Were you planning on joining us this morning?" asked Jason, with a good-humored smile. He looked like he had had a full night's sleep.

"I overslept," she said, running her hands through her tousled hair. "You go on without me. I'll grab a quick shower and meet you there." As she closed the door, she noticed a piece of paper on the floor by the stoop. She picked it up and unfolded the hotel stationery. It was a note from Michel.

Darn, she thought, *how could I have overslept?* She wanted to cry for the missed opportunity of saying goodbye and of wishing him good luck on his show. He had done so much for her and she had failed even this little courtesy.

I wish I could stay to see your success, but I know that you will knock 'em dead. Good luck. I'll be thinking of you.

Michel

So much left unsaid. Kara crumpled the page and then thought better of it. She flattened it out and tucked it inside her appointment book. She showered and dressed quickly, and then waited impatiently while the doorman hailed her a taxi. She looked forward to a busy day, not for the benefit of In-A-Wink, but for her. The busier she was, the less time she would have to pine for Michel.

Chapter Eight

In the days following her return from Germany, Kara often thought of Michel. She wondered about his show in New York and wished that she had his phone number there. She also wondered why he didn't call, though he had told her not to expect it. Still, she did. Through all of the excitement of the last days of Photokina, Kara had not had much time to enjoy her memories of their brief time together. Now her days were taken up with meeting new contacts and negotiating for the Christmas season. But her nights . . . her nights were empty. Monica tried to fix her up with third cousins and Annie insisted that she should join a health club, if for no other reason than to meet others of her own age. She'd even been flirted with at the all-night supermarket, and yet none of these possible encounters interested her.

On the first cold day in October, when she still had not heard from Michel, she began to worry. She still felt guilty about not saying goodbye and wanted to make it up to him.

She lit a fire in her living room and curled up in its warmth with a book, but she couldn't read.

There are many things that you don't know about me, Kara. Michel's voice echoed in her mind. Where was he now? Did he remember the feeling of having her in his arms beneath the great gothic towers of the Dom? Did he care? She would have picked up the phone then and there had she known his number in New York. She stared at the wireless phone receiver cradled in her lap, willing it to ring.

This is foolish, she thought, feeling like a schoolgirl, waiting for a call after her first date. But she knew that it was much worse than that. She was in love with Michel. He had pushed her away many times, as if he feared getting too close, but she thought that in Germany he had finally come around. The way he had touched her hair and kissed her pointed to strong feelings on his part.

So why hadn't he called.

Even as she dialed his number, she knew that she was doing the wrong thing. Michel had said that he would call when he returned to Montreal, and if he was home and hadn't yet called, well then, that should speak volumes about his intentions, and she should just hang up right now.

It rang three times. Kara imagined him out in the garden, rushing for the phone, or in his studio, so deep in concentration that he didn't even hear it ring.

He never did show me his studio, she thought, remembering his reluctance to bring her there. Did he trust her enough now to let her into that private place?

After seven rings the answering machine picked up.

"You have reached Michel Vernier. Please leave a message." The recording was repeated in French. She hung up the phone without a word. She had never heard him speak in his native tongue before, and suddenly she was struck by the great divide between them. He was a French artist, from a wealthy Senneville family. She was an Anglophone businesswoman who had grown up in Montreal's poorest district. How could she have felt so close to a man whose whole existence was the opposite of her own? The panic she felt at these thoughts almost undid her. She had devoted so much energy to a relationship that didn't even exist.

She picked up the phone again, determined this time to leave a message, any message, but she put the receiver down without dialing.

That's just about enough childish antics for one night, she thought, turning back to her book, but the evening turned into night and the fire died down to glowing embers before Kara had even turned a page.

The next day Kara took action. It had been three weeks since she returned from Photokina. Michel should have returned from New York a week ago.

She convinced herself that her anxiety had more to do with his safety than with her feelings of rejection.

She decided to call the Westmount Gallery. Hopefully, André-Guy Bernard would know if Michel had returned. While she waited for the receptionist to put her through, Kara stilled her nerves by flicking the pages of her appointment book. If she could pretend that this was a business call, she could get through it with only minor discomfort.

"*Allo*?" André-Guy sounded as bored as ever.

"Mr. Bernard?" asked Kara uncertainly.

"*Oui*."

"Uh, yes. My name is Kara Mackenzie. We met at the opening of Michel Vernier's last exhibit."

"*Oui*." He was not making this easy.

"Well, I've been trying to contact Mr. Vernier for several days. I was wondering if you could tell me how to get in touch with him."

There was a muffled pause, as if he had covered the mouthpiece with his hand while he consulted with someone in the room.

"Yes, Miss Mackenzie. Monsieur Vernier told me to inform you that he stayed on in New York to promote a second show."

"Oh." Kara didn't know what to say. "Well, do you know when he'll be back?"

"That will depend on whether or not the show is a success, won't it? Good day, Miss Mackenzie."

Even the click of his hanging up sounded snooty. She spent several minutes just banging her pen against her appointment book trying to cool her anger. Oh, she disliked that man!

Monsieur Vernier *told* him to say? Something in his tone sounded off, as if Michel had been standing right beside André-Guy while he spoke to her. Michel might have told him to say it, but that didn't mean it was the truth. And if it was, then why didn't Michel tell her himself?

Kara finally had to face the fact that Michel was avoiding her. He wasn't in New York. He was sitting in André-Guy's office having a good laugh at her expense. She should go over to the gallery and confront him. She was angry and embarrassed, and the more she thought about it, the more angry she became simply because he had the power to embarrass her. Even Matthew at his worst, when he had forced her to call security, had not embarrassed her like this.

With a sinking heart, she knew that she would never confront Michel. Why should she? So that he could tell her to her face that he did not love her, that he hadn't even thought about her since Germany, that she didn't fit into his exciting artist's life? She already knew these things. His silence spoke louder than words. She couldn't think about it anymore, not at the office when tears threatened to spill out of her eyes and drown all the papers on her desk. Not when everyone could see her distress and know that, once again, she had picked the wrong man.

Disgusted with herself, she pushed the phone away and picked up a fax that had just come in. At least it was good news. The manufacturers of Prolar lenses had been so impressed with their marketing at Photokina that they were offering her the exclusive North American rights to their line. That meant their market had just increased tenfold. It meant new jobs and probably even a new office down south.

Silently, Kara thanked Arthur and Clyde once again. Their antics had even caught the attentions of the journalist who recorded the everyday happenings of Photokina in the daily newspaper. In-A-Wink had received a very favorable writeup, citing their ''sense of flair and fun'' for setting a new trend in the look of the photo industry, ''an industry that has for too long been too impressed with its own seriousness.''

After that, the crowds to their booth had been unending. More than once, Kara had caught Matthew looking over at them enviously, but he had caused no further problems. Perhaps he had finally accepted that Kara was out of his reach.

She had met many American buyers at the show. These new contacts would form the backbone of their U.S. market share. It was just one more thing that Kara wished to thank Michel for. She buzzed Chloe and told her to get Harvey, her lawyer, on the line.

She was glad to have something to occupy her mind and her hands. She pushed her heartache to the back of her thoughts, where it simmered steadily. Who had time for love anyway, when there was a whole continent to conquer?

When Kara had given Harvey enough details to get the ball rolling, she hung up and paged Annie.

"I'm meeting Harvey for dinner," said Kara, not looking up from her appointment book. "He has a preliminary contract for the lensticks, and we're breaking into the American market with Prolar. I'm going to see if we can get an exclusive on the lenstick, too. It might already be too late, but I'll bully them."

"Wow," said Annie. "We're quite the shark."

"We've got clout now, and we've got to push ahead while the memory of Photokina is still fresh in their minds. I'd like you to be there tonight. Can you make it?"

"Of course," said Annie. "Did you think I'd have a hot date?" Kara nodded. She was intently rereading the fax and had not even heard Annie's response.

Annie watched her with interest. Kara's mouth was pinched in a tight line. Her brow was furrowed with concentration, and yet she seemed to read the same paragraph over and over again. Something was going on, something that had nothing to do with lenses.

"You, on the other hand," said Annie, "should have a hot date, and I don't mean with your lawyer."

Kara finally looked up.

"Huh?"

"A certain artist perhaps. I hear that he has returned from New York a success."

Kara stared at Annie blankly while the bile churned in her stomach. Returned from New York? She almost asked how Annie knew, but with her worst suspicions confirmed she didn't care to know any more.

"I've more important concerns," snapped Kara, "like saving our company from bankruptcy."

If Annie was shocked by Kara's tone, she said nothing. She knew better than to push her.

Left alone in her office again, Kara sought solace planning her coming month down to the minute. At five o'clock she put everything away, and resigned herself to an evening of Harvey's bad jokes and Annie's worried looks. It was better than spending the night alone.

Kara spent the next month in planes and taxis, meeting with American buyers as well as interviewing prospective salespeople. In the new year all the red tape would be sorted out and In-A-Wink would open its first American office. In the meantime, Annie ran the fort in Montreal while Kara struggled to hang onto the contacts that she had made in Germany. With this hectic pace, Kara had had little time to think about her crushed hopes. She had yet to grieve for her lost love.

Kara knew that Annie worried about her. Kara was worried about herself when she had the time to think about it. She had lost weight. When she looked in the mirror, her cheeks were hollow and her eyes . . . well, she didn't care to look at herself in the eye.

She pretended that the memories of Michel were fading, but sometimes at night, as she lay awake in yet another strange hotel, an image of him would surface in her mind—an image so sharp, so real, that he might be standing right before her. Or she would hear his voice and the deep rumble of his laugh, a laugh that had come so easily when they had been together.

Many times she asked herself how she could have been so wrong. Had she read too much into his embraces? Did he kiss every woman he met like that? Always she came back to the same thought: she hadn't been wrong. He had cared for her. But then why had he so effectively cut her out of his life?

In her dreams, she called him a hundred times, using an old rotary phone. Each time, her finger slipped on the last number, and the operator would tell her to try her call again. She would bang down the phone and wake up in the darkness, tears of frustration choking her.

She also dreamed of loving him, though when she woke, she could only remember the curve of his bare shoulder, stretched taut, as he wrapped his arms around her. And his eyes. They looked down on her with a fire or was that the sparkle of mockery?

She had resigned herself to never seeing him again, but it would be a long time before she exorcised his memory from the sanctuary of her desires.

As Christmas approached, Kara put her traveling on hold. Most retailers had blown their Christmas budgets by this time, and they concentrated on selling the stock. The quiet time at the office was particularly painful to Kara. She had spent last Christmas alone, after her breakup with Matthew, and had rather enjoyed it, but this year would be different. Annie would, of course, invite her to spend the day with her family, but Kara wasn't sure that she could take all the shouting and cheering that went with Annie's extended family and twelve grandchildren.

Besides, she should spend Christmas with her mother. During her frequent trips down south, Kara had constantly checked in with Monica and Dr. Hanson. Monica's moods were getting worse, and Kara, with her own problems, was becoming increasingly impatient with her. In her heart, Kara knew that her mother suffered from feelings of neglect and low self-esteem, but she was tired of being responsible for her. Monica was a grown woman. Her refusal seek professional help was selfish and childish, and Kara had decided not to cater to such behavior anymore.

On a Friday afternoon in early December, she went home early to pack her bags. She had one last trip to Vancouver to make, as a special favor to a longtime client. She had an hour to kill before calling the taxi. She made a pot of tea and called her mother.

"Kara, darling! How are you?" Monica's voice lilted and slurred. She sounded positively cheery.

"Mother, have you been drinking?" Kara immediately regretted her accusing tone, but Monica only laughed.

"Don't be silly. It's only three o'clock."

"Are you feeling okay?"

"Oh, just wonderful. Dr. Hanson passed by yesterday and gave me some new medication. Little pick-me-uppers, if you know what I mean.''

So Dr. Hanson had finally conceded to the antidepressants.

Things must be worse than I thought. Kara made a note to call the doctor and find out what he had prescribed. She wanted to know if she should expect any nasty side effects.

''I'm leaving tonight for one more show in Vancouver, Mom. Will you be okay?''

''Of course, dear. Off to lick your wounds, are you?''

''Lick my wounds? I'm going on business, Mom. What do you mean?'' Kara assumed that she was talking about Matthew. Monica had finally understood that Matthew was out of her life for good. Making her understand that Kara liked it that way, was another matter.

''I mean your painter friend, you foolish girl.'' Suddenly Monica's voice was very clear, as if she wanted Kara to understand every word. Warning bells sounded in Kara's mind. Her mother's cheeriness was deceptive. She braced herself for a row. In this mood, Monica's spite knew no bounds, and no one was safe from it, least of all her daughter. Later, when the funk lifted, Monica would beg for Kara's forgiveness. She would promise never to be so cruel again, but none of it mattered to Kara anymore. She refused to be a punching bag any longer.

''What about Michel?'' sighed Kara. She had given Monica only the briefest details about their short relationship and subsequent breakup, but that hadn't stopped Monica from harping on the subject.

"Well." Karla could tell that Monica was smirking. There was something that she was dying to say, and reluctantly, Kara's curiosity was piqued. "You must have been shocked to find out that your rich artist lover is a fraud."

"He's not my lover," said Kara automatically.

"Well, whatever. He's a liar and a fraud. Mansion in Senneville, like heck. He's been lying to you all this time, or did you know already and just not want to tell your nagging mother?"

"Know what, Mom? I have no idea what you are talking about."

"That's what happens to women who join the business world," said Monica, her voice full of pity, "they start to think like men and lose all their feminine instinct. Open your newspaper to the arts and entertainment section. It's all there. Michel Vernier is a fraud. He's an out-of-work bum who thinks he's got something worth saying to the world. Honestly, Kara, I can't believe you were stupid enough to fall for that."

Kara absorbed her mother's words for several long seconds.

"Forget the lecture, Mom. Just tell me what you're talking about."

"There's an article about starving artists in to-day's newspaper. Don't tell me that an important businesswoman like yourself doesn't read the newspaper."

Kara marveled at the way, in a few short sentences, Monica could encapsulate all her bitterness about Kara's life choices: the fact that Kara had chosen a career over family, that she could not be admitted to Kara's business world, and that Kara never confided in her mother.

In fact, Kara hadn't read the day's paper. It was folded in her briefcase, being saved for the long flight to Vancouver. That none of her staff, especially Annie, had pointed the article out to her, indicated what they thought of Kara's emotional state.

"They've done a really interesting piece on the local art scene," said Monica, clearly relishing her drama. "A destitute bunch, the lot of them. They even talk about your Mr. Vernier. Picture of him, too. He is a doll. Clearly you were thinking with your hormones or you would have seen that he was a total fraud. Well, anyway I'm sure you don't care, rushing off to Vancouver and all. Probably don't want to be bothered with your crabby old mother anyway. Bye-bye. Have a safe trip."

The line clicked dead.

Kara hated the way her mother left no room for retaliation. She wanted to call her back and demand an explanation, but she could not resist pulling the newspaper out of her briefcase.

Ignoring the headlines, she skipped right to the arts section. On the cover was a color photo of Michel. He seemed to be looking right at her and Kara's stomach did a little dance. How could this man continue to get under her skin?

Only after several minutes of staring at the photo did she realize that he was standing in his studio, the studio that she had so much wanted to see. The photo was not very clear, but she could make out a small cluttered room. It was not the studio that she had imagined. She had pictured a brightly lit wing of the Senneville house, with large windows overlooking the garden.

She remembered Monica's words: *Mansion in Senneville, like heck!*

The caption to the photo read: Starving for Art. With a sense of foreboding, Kara continued with the article. When she was done she poured herself another cup of tea. It was only tepid now, but she didn't taste it anyway. She pushed herself away from the table, away from Michel's smiling face. But everywhere she looked she could see him. He was standing at her sink, elbow deep in soapy water. She walked out to the patio and he was there, leaning against the wall where they had chatted so long ago.

"Liar!" she cried, slamming the tea cup against the brick wall. She had kept the hurt in for so long that she was stunned by her own violent outburst. She sat in a deck chair, though it was cold and wet with snow, and cried.

It was all a lie, his caresses and kind words. Over the weeks she had almost convinced herself that it was her fault that he had left her. She had been selfish and unable to share his life with him, when he had given her so much. Somehow, blaming herself had made things easier. At least it was some explanation. And now she realized that no matter how good or loving she could have been it would have ended the same way. He never had any intentions of pursuing their relationship.

"When we get closer," he had said in the gazebo, "I don't want it to be because you are too upset by your past to make the right decision." It seemed so mocking now. Why hadn't he just said "I don't want you"?

With a bout of masochism, Kara returned to the kitchen table to reread the newspaper article.

"After his success in New York," she read and thought that at least that much had been true. He had gone to New York, though she was now certain that he had also been in André-Guy's office, directing his words.

"After his success in New York, Michel Vernier returns to his tiny apartment in one of Montreal's poorest districts." If it hadn't been for the photo, Kara would have wondered who she was reading about. "Even success in New York, the capital of the art world, doesn't always mean financial success." Kara couldn't help wondering if the reporter was the same pretty blond who had hung on to Michel at the Westmount Gallery. The byline—J. D. Cruishank—told her nothing. She read on.

Michel Vernier is Montreal's hottest new talent. His work has been shown in Paris and New York. Critics hail him as a hybrid between Robert Bateman and Van Gogh and more passion-

ate that both. But like Van Gogh, must he live
his life in poverty, finding success—as mea-
sured by dollar sales—only after his death?

   Despite the poor surroundings of his tiny east
end studio, Vernier is optimistic.

   "It's not a life for everyone," he stresses,
"but I love what I do. I get by."

Get by! thought Kara. Was this the same man who
had poured her sparkling water on a gazebo in Senneville? Was this the man who dressed with a style
that only those born with class could mimic?

However, certain of his oddities now became
clear, such as why he never allowed her to see he
studio, and why she never actually saw him drive his
own car.

The man she had fallen in love with was a myth.
Not because her illusions of living the high life in a
Senneville mansion had been shattered, but because
all the tender words he ever uttered to her now rang
with deceit. She didn't know whom that house be-
longed to, but right now it didn't matter. Whatever
the twisted story was, Michel had lied to her.

The rest of the article talked about his work, de-
scribing many of the paintings that Kara had seen at
the Montreal exhibit. In conclusion, Michel returned
to the theme of monetary success, as if to drive home
to Kara that she had been duped.

"Art collectors are finicky," he was quoted as
saying. "They invest a lot of money in their collec-
tions and they want to be guaranteed a return. I can't

do that. All I can do is capture their imaginations and hope for the best.''

The reporter asked what Michel's plans were for the future and he answered that he would always paint.

''It's like breathing to me, but I would like to gain more than critical success. Stability is important to me. I'd like to have a family one day.''

The reporter concluded the piece with: ''When asked if there was anyone special in his life, Michel just waved his brush with true artistic manner and said, 'Every starving artist has a secret passion. That's what fires my brush.' But he would say no more. Perhaps his paintbrush will.''

Kara wasn't surprised that Michel had never mentioned any past love to her. While she had opened herself up to him, he had kept his own private life classified. If she hadn't felt so betrayed, she would have been sorry for him. He lived the life of a tragic hero.

She left the paper open on the table. She left the shards of teacup scattered on the patio. She would deal with it all later. She bundled herself in a knitted blanket and curled up on her couch in the living room. The sky was already darkening and she realised that she had missed her flight to Vancouver. She would call them tomorrow and apologize. It was not an important trip, anyway. Kara had only planned it so that she wouldn't have to be alone this weekend, but now she wanted nothing more than to sit here in the dark, alone.

Though she now new the truth, there were still many things that didn't make any sense. She thought about the evening that they had spent in the gazebo on top of the fairy knoll. He had been so gentle, so caring. Why, if he had only been playing games with her, had he not made a pass at her then? Why had he not just tried to use her? He'd had the chance. She had made herself available, and yet he had held back. Unless, of course, she repulsed him all together, but she knew that wasn't true. The memories of his touch, so passionate and searching, were still vivid in her memory.

It wasn't just the memory of his actions that pained her, though. She had opened up to him, had told him things that she had told no other, and yet, he hadn't trusted her. Did he think so little of her that he couldn't tell her where he lived? Did he think she would look down on him? Kara might be considered rich by some standards, but she had worked hard all her life. She had grown up in that same poor neighborhood where Michel now had his studio. She had watched her father struggle to make a better life for them. She had put herself through college and then, for many years, while In-A-Wink gained its wings, she had lived hand to mouth. In-A-Wink was her artwork. Maybe that's why she had felt so close to him. Despite the very different worlds they lived in, they both struggled to build something meaningful, something lasting, with the talents they had. Only Michel didn't know these things about her. He hadn't taken the chance to know them.

Kara remembered how out of place she had felt at the Westmount Gallery, surrounded by the fashionable art dealers and critics. She thought that she didn't fit in, but really she did. She now understood what it must be like each time Michel sold one of his paintings. That same sense of pride that she felt each time she made a good deal, or planned a successful marketing campaign. A sense of pride, yes, but also an overwhelming relief, to know where the next paycheck was coming form. And how much more poignant that relief must be to Michel. Each painting sold was a little piece of himself gone, but it also meant the chance to buy more paint and canvas to create another, in the hopes that one day all these little pieces of himself would gain him the stability that he craved.

It was ironic that he spoke of stability, and yet, since he came into her life, she had been unbalanced as never before. Even Matthew's betrayal had not confused her like this.

Oh dear, she thought. *That's it*. Michel didn't want anyone to have to live with his instability. That's why he kept pushing her away. Kara knew what it was like to be responsible for others. She had agonized over possible downsizing before Christmas. Maybe Michel felt that he couldn't be responsible for anyone else, and so he preferred to be alone. He never gave her the chance to choose her own fate. Better to do the rejecting than be the rejected. She suspected that his pride had come between them and was sorry that she had not confronted him right away. Her own fear of rejection had held her back. But no more. Michel could not hurt her any more than he already had. She might be wrong. Michel might have pushed her away because he just didn't love her, but Kara knew that she could never live with herself if she didn't find out for sure.

For the first time in many weeks, she dared to have hope. There were still many unanswered questions, starting with who really lived in that mansion in Senneville, but tomorrow she would get some answers.

In the meantime, she had one more bit of unfinished business. It was completely dark now, but she didn't turn on a light. Her mind was focused, and she didn't want the distractions of the world around her to intrude. She picked up the phone and dialed Monica's number.

After several rings, the answering machine picked up, but that was all right. What Kara had to say would take less than a minute.

"Mom, it's Kara. I just read the article about Michel and you were right: I was foolish to take him at face value. I wish I was calling to get some motherly advice, but I see now that your spite will always come between us. I was very hurt to know that Michel lied to me, but not as hurt as when I realized that you took pleasure in my pain. I hope Dr. Hanson is able to help you, because I can't any longer." Kara paused. She wanted to add that Monica shouldn't call her unless she sought the help she needed, but she couldn't bring herself to say the words. "Bye, Mom," was all she could manage before the answering machine cut her off. She put down the phone. Relief and sorrow battled for control of her emotions, but it was a night for resolutions, and she decided that Monica's childish spite would no longer be a part of her life.

She loved her mother and would always welcome her into her life, but from now on she would stand up for herself. For too long she had made excuses for Monica, but no more. She would have to learn responsibility for her actions, and maybe, Kara dared to hope, that responsibility would spur her to get the help she needed.

Kara was strangely exhilarated. She felt in control of her future for the first time in many months. It was still early, but she went to bed anyway and fell into a dreamless, untroubled sleep.

Chapter Nine

Kara rang the doorbell quickly before she lost her nerve. The first time she had visited Senneville it had been dark. The house and grounds were even more splendid in the daylight. Kara quelled the urge to skip around the house and find the fairy knoll. After a brief wait, an elderly gentleman answered the door. He bore little resemblance to Michel. His face was long, his hair gray, but his eyes were unmistakeably Vernier.

"I'm looking for Michel Vernier," stuttered Kara.

The man raised an eyebrow and said, "He's not in." He was clearly Francophone, but he spoke English with a faint British accent as if he had been educated in England.

"Are you his father?" Her question was rather blunt, but she had come this far and was not going home without some answers.

"I'm his brother, actually."

Kara flushed in embarrassment, but he held up his hand in protest.

"Don't worry, it's a common mistake. Won't you come in, Miss . . . ?"

"Mackenzie. Kara Mackenzie." He smiled at her.

"Won't you come in, Miss Mackenzie? You seem distraught."

She followed him into a sitting room.

"My name is Louis." He indicated that she should sit by the fire.

Kara smiled shakily and nodded. Louis poured two small glasses of iced tea and sat in a wingback chair opposite her. A large white cat watched them sleepily from the hearth. Two others, one black and one tortoiseshell, were stretched along the back of a couch against one wall. As soon as she sat down, the black cat jumped off the couch and joined her in the chair. Without introductions, he settled himself on her lap like a warm, purring comforter.

"That's Monty," said Louis. "You don't mind, do you? Just push him off . . ."

"No," said Kara, stroking his soft fur. "He's fine, really." The smooth vibrations of his purr calmed her. Louis nodded with approval.

"I won't ask if you are a friend of my brother, because clearly you are or you wouldn't be looking for him. And clearly you're not, or you would know that Michel hasn't lived here for years."

"But I was here with him!" Kara blurted, and then realized that maybe she maybe she shouldn't have said anything.

"Mmm." He sipped his drink. "Last summer was that?" Kara nodded. "Yes, I found Michel at my breakfast table, and two unwashed glasses on the counter. Frankly, I was surprised. I have offered Michel free run of the manor for years, but that was the first time that he actually took me up on the suggestion.''

There was an awkward pause while both Louis and Kara were preoccupied with their own memories of Michel. Finally Kara realized that her host, though too polite to ask, was waiting for her to explain her presence.

"I'm sorry, Mr. Vernier . . ."

"Please call me Louis."

"Louis . . . I must seem very strange to you."

"Well, you do appear rather lost, but then caring for stray kittens has become a sort of hobby for me. So take your time." He reached across the space separating them and refilled her glass. The iced tea had soothed her, but she had not meant to gulp it. She sipped the second glass more slowly.

"You see," she started, trying to make sense of this mess, "Michel told me that this was his house."

"He did?" Louis raised his expressive eyebrows in surprise.

"Well, actually," Kara frowned. She tried to remember exactly what he had said. "He said that he had grown up here. He called it the family manor, and because there was nobody else here, I assumed that it was his."

"And he let you assume."

"Yes. Why would he do that?"

"I'm not sure. Michel hasn't wanted anything to

do with this house for years. I can only suggest that you, Miss Kara, had some impact on him.''

''Right,'' said Kara, not hiding the bitterness from her voice. ''I had such an impact on him, that I scared him into hiding for three months.''

Louis stared at her thoughtfully for a moment. Monty moaned in his sleep, as if her words disturbed him. Absently, Kara stroked him from head to tail, and he slept on.

''Well,'' asked Louis, finally. ''Why, after three months, did you show up here today?''

''The article in yesterday's paper,'' said Kara miserably.

''Oh, yes. The starving artist of Montreal. A fascinating piece, for sure. Was that the first time you realized that Michel had lied to you?'' Kara nodded. ''But why, Miss Kara, after all this time did you wish to pursue the matter? Out of vengeance?''

''No!'' she blurted. Monty opened one eye at her outburst. ''Not anything like that. It's just that I need to understand. He cut himself off so quickly, so thoroughly . . . I just . . . I just love him, still.'' The last words were quiet and she would not look Louis in the eye when she said them. Instead she concentrated on the few tufts of white fur on Monty's back. When she finally looked up, Louis grinned at her.

''Well,'' he said, ''that is what I wanted to hear. Now I can tell you that my brother has the unforgivable habit of running away from his problems.''

''I didn't realize that I was a problem.''

''Nor are you,'' continued Louis, ''no more than I am a problem to Michel, or my father before me.

We are all just people who care about him. Unfortunately, Michel finds caring difficult, not that he cares any less than the rest of us. In fact, I think that when Michel loves someone his love is so strong that it becomes a burden to him. His greatest fear is to let down those he loves by being inadequate, and yet that fear is what keeps him away from us, and ironically, what lets us down.

"You see, Michel was a retirement present for my father, really. I came home one Christmas—it was my last year at university—to find my father remarried and expecting a baby." Louis chuckled at the memory. "It was pleasure to see him—usually so severe—finally enjoying life. He had always been a workaholic, building his father's small business into an empire. But I guess that when he met Elyse, he discovered that there was more important things in life. I was happy for him, and I adored Elyse. She was more like a little sister to me than a stepmother.

"By the time Michel was born, I had returned from school for good and had started taking over my father's duties as the head of the company. Father took off many afternoons and long weekends to be with his young family. I encouraged him. He was not a well man, by that time, and Elyse's eyes lit up when he entered the room. They spent all their time with Michel, as a baby, a toddler and then a very active child. He was never alone, and they never relied on babysitters. If a restaurant would not allow children, they found another restaurant.

"You know," he said, almost wistfully, "they say

that a troubled childhood stays with you all your life, but so does a blissful one. And when that bliss is taken away, it can be an insurmountable grief. When Michel was barely seven years old, Elyse died suddenly.''

Louis took a gulp of his drink. He seemed lost in his tale, and Kara wondered if he even remembered that she was there.

''A big part of my father died that day, too. Unable to cope with his own misery, let alone that of a child, he sent Michel away to boarding school. For seven years Michel had been the center of this household. I can only imagine what an adjustment that must have been for him.''

Kara could almost feel the boy's grief, and yet she couldn't relate this small, lost child to Michel, who always seemed so confident and at ease with himself. *And yet,* she thought, *I know now that he is not, or else he wouldn't have pushed me away.* She remembered the look he had given her when they parted on her front stoop after the staff party. He had wanted so much to say something. His eyes had been full of sadness, and in that look Kara had glimpsed, unknowingly, that lost child.

''He didn't do well in school,'' continued Louis, ''constantly causing disruptions, being rude to teachers. He fell in with a bad crowd, and I think there were drugs involved.

''In one of the rare moments that Michel actually confided in me, he said that school was boring and that all his teachers were small-minded bureaucrats.''

Louis laughed. "Can you imagine? He was fifteen, but I remember thinking at the time he might be a little snob, but he was smarter than any of us and he was falling through the cracks of the education system.

"I suggested to Father that Michel should be sent to Europe to study art. He clearly had the talent, and I thought the Europeans would be more tolerant of his eccentricities. Unfortunately," he grimaced, "my kind thought backfired. Father accused me of wanting to turn Michel into some kind of free-loading hippie. These were the seventies, remember, and when Michel heard about the fuss, he accused me of trying to get rid of him."

Kara felt sorry for Louis, though he told the story as if it were just that, a story that could have happened to anyone.

"You must be surprised that I'm telling you all this, Miss Kara." She nodded. "You might think that I'm just an old man who likes to spin tales, which is not entirely untrue, but these things happened so long ago, that even Michel has, to some extent, dealt with them. Nonetheless, they stayed with him, became part of his makeup, and if you wish to understand Michel, you need to hear it all. I'm not being too forthright am I?"

"No," said Kara. "You're right. I need to hear the rest."

"Well, of course, it was a ridiculous idea that I wanted to be rid of him. Really, just a product of his inflated ego. I was already the president of Father's company. What did I need to fear from a sixteen-year-old boy who was really nothing more than a hood?

"But when Michel gets an idea in his head, he takes it all the way. I believe that you have already noticed this about my dear brother. He accused me of all kinds of wild things: jealousy, spitefulness, manipulation. I was shocked. He had so much anger bottled inside him.

"Father intervened on my behalf and that's when the argument gained apocalyptic proportions. The two had hardly spoken since Michel was a child, and they could not begin now. They shouted at each other for half an hour, neither one listening to the other, only trying to make himself heard. Finally, Michel started packing his bags. Father uttered those fateful words: If he left, Michel shouldn't bother coming back, because there would be no home for him here. He would be disinherited.

"That seemed to be just the push that Michel needed, but he was not quite out the door when Father had his heart attack. He did not survive the ride to the hospital."

"Oh, no," whispered Kara.

"Yes," said Louis, "I agree. The guilt must have been overwhelming, but I didn't blame Michel. Father was a stubborn old man. Michel was only a child. Father should have known better. I should have known better . . ." Louis shook his head, as if the memories clouded his thoughts.

"Michel was not at the funeral or the reading of

the will. Of course Father had not had time to disinherit him, and in my heart, I know that he would not have done so anyway. Michel was entitled to half of everything.'' He waved his hand as if to encompass the house and everything in it.

"When I finally found him, living in some hovel downtown, I begged him to come home, but he was adamant. 'My father's last wishes will be honored,' he said.

"Poor kid, I thought, and yet he was no longer a kid. In the space of a few months he had grown up. His rebelliousness had turned into resoluteness. He had hardened, though he had mellowed a bit, too. He accepted my offers for dinner as long as it was at a restaurant. And he let me buy him some equipment for his studio. For that, I was grateful. I had worried that my interference would turn him off painting altogether, but I understand now, that this is impossible. Painting is his life. He could no more give it up than you or I could give up fresh air.

"Over the years I have used my influence to help out his career now and then. I'm sure that Michel is aware of my minor interferences, though he has never mentioned them. He comes to visit me now. I think the ghosts of this house are finally put to rest for him. But I still hold his inheritance in trust for him, or perhaps for his children.'' He sipped from his glass, and continued. "Michel does not enjoy living like a pauper. All of his childhood friends deserted him, not understanding his lifestyle choice. Do you, Miss Kara, understand?''

Kara thought about it for a moment. Louis was testing her, and she didn't want to sound flippant.

"I think so," she said finally. "Michel wants to find the security that he had as a child, but his pride demands that he does it on his own, without your father's money." Louis nodded at her, like a benevolent teacher to his pupil.

Kara remembered the lone character in Michel's paintings, each a witness to some awesome power that he could not control, each in some way that abandoned child.

"Why didn't he tell me this himself?" she asked.

"Michel would not thank us for dissecting his psyche like this. He has a great sense of pride, Miss Kara. He's had to. It's the only thing that has kept him alive all these years. That and his art. My guess is that now he's met someone who matters more than both of those and that scares him."

Louis let these revelations sink in.

"How can you be so sure of that?" she asked after several moments.

"That morning after you were here, I inquired about the two glasses, not actually expecting Michel to confide in me about his love life, but he described you in the most intriguing terms, flattery that I now see you truly merit." Kara tried to accept the compliments with grace, but she flushed faintly.

"I expressed my dismay at having missed your visit, and Michel assured me that I would meet you one day. Again, he was right. You must understand, Miss Kara, Michel has never wanted me to meet his

friends before, female or otherwise. I believe that
you kindle a sort of family spirit in him.''

Suddenly Kara was fired with determination. She
sat upright, dumping the disgruntled Monty on the
floor.

''Will you tell me where he lives?'' she asked.

''Of course I will.'' As they both stood up, Louis
took her hand in his own and led her to the front
door. ''But I'm afraid that Michel won't like you
intruding there. You're going to have to battle his
pride, and believe me, that is no easy task.''

Kara nodded. She knew that an unpleasant confrontation lay ahead of her, but she was armed with
knowledge now, and that was ever so much better
than sitting in the darkness of ignorance as she had
done for so many months now.

As they said their good-byes, Kara felt as if she
were leaving an old friend.

*Why do these Vernier men have such an effect of
me?* she wondered.

''Please,'' said Louis, ''let me know what happens, one way or the other. Michel will surely never
say, and well, I worry about my baby brother still.''

Kara promised to call and then on a whim, she
asked Louis is she could take a walk around the garden before leaving. She wanted to see the fairy hill
again.

''Fairy hill?'' he asked with a bewildered smile.

''Yes, the hill with the gazebo.''

''I know what you mean. It's just . . .'' he grinned

at her, and he dropped ten years in an instant. ''Elyse used to call it that: the fairy hill.''

Kara kissed him on the cheek, and walked around to the back of the house, hoping to find some inspiration from the fairies in the knoll.

Chapter Ten

Kara approached Michel's building with mounting apprehension. Louis' encouragement had fired her determination, but now that she was here, standing in front of a crumbling apartment in the less than savory east end, she was having second thoughts. She paused at the glass door that led to a dim entryway. The lock had been ripped off. There was a foul odor in the air that Kara didn't wish to put a name to.

She now understood why Michel had reacted so harshly when she had invited herself to see his studio, but that didn't make the sting of his rejection any kinder. She hadn't spoken to him in so long now, he might have forgotten her. Or worse, what if he wasn't alone? What if there was another woman upstairs with him?

She bit her lip with indecision. Memories, good and bad, fought for dominion over her head and heart: The muffled sound of André-Guy covering the

174

phone while he consulted with someone, presumably Michel. The comforting feel of his arms around her after he had rejected her advances in the gazebo. The flash of jealousy in his eyes when she came home late in Cologne. The sound of his voice in her ear as she lay against him, staring up at the six-hundred-year-old cathedral.

She remembered the way he often kissed her on the top of her head, or just beside her mouth as if denying himself—and her—that final pleasure of claiming her lips.

All of these memories assailed her, but none of them could make her open that door and head up the gloomy stairwell. In the past few months, Kara had overcome many obstacles. In-A-Wink was once again a leader in the photographic industry. Matthew's company was flailing in her wake, but more important, he no longer had the power to hurt her. She had resolved to let Monica's problems be her own, and had put that resolve into action. Annie would be proud of her. When this was all over, one way or another, they would have a very long spaghetti dinner, but right now, Kara had to force herself to open that door and confront Michel.

What finally urged her on was the simple memory of Michel massaging her shoulders as they sat at the foot of the Dom. He had listened to her worries then, just like he had in the gazebo, and yet she had never asked him about his own troubles. He had been a friend when she most needed one. He had listened without judgment, and she wanted, if nothing else, to show him that she could do the same.

His apartment was three flights up. She ignored the peeling walls and stained floors. Without a thought, she stepped over a broken stair. When she reached his door, there was no bell. She knocked, a timid sound in the silent building. After a few minutes she knocked again, louder this time.

The door was flung open. The moment he saw her, Michel's expression changed from irritation to bewilderment.

"Kara!" It was not a question, but an exclamation of dismay. He wore a ragged denim shirt spotted with paint. His beard was at least two days old, and his eyes were red-rimmed, as if he had worked through the night. He stared at her dumbly, as if she were a ghost come back from the dead. She thought that he looked absolutely beautiful.

"May I come in?" she asked after a few moments of awkward silence. Michel held the door wide and motioned her inside. It was like stepping into another world. The newspaper photo had made it seem small and chaotic, but his studio was as bright as the hallway had been dingy. There were only two windows at one end, but they were large enough to light the whole loft. Several plants cheered the severe brick walls. A smell of turpentine, laced with coffee, permeated the room. Michel walked over to a pot on an electric warmer.

"Would you like a cup of coffee?" he asked.

Kara nodded. She was still busy taking in her surroundings, as if she had found a sunlit glade in the middle of a daunting forest. A wooden worktable, littered with paint tubes, jars, and other tools, covered the left wall. Beside it, turned toward the window so that Kara couldn't see it properly, was an easel with a half-finished canvas. She resisted the urge to peek at it. There were plenty of others to see. Canvasses lined the walls, stacked three deep. Portraits, and landscapes, still lifes, and some that Kara could only describe as abstract. The room was a riot of color.

She made her way to where an old plush couch and a couple of recliners were positioned to make a sort of living room. She sat on the couch as Michel joined her with the coffee. He perched on the arm of one chair, indicating that this interview would only last a few minutes. From over the rim of his mug, he regarded her with dark eyes.

"I've been reading about you in the paper," said Kara, cautiously. Michel didn't respond, but only continued to glare at her. Kara couldn't tell if his belligerence was heartfelt or if he used it to mask another emotion.

"You could imagine my surprise when I discovered that you didn't live in Senneville."

"Disappointed, were you?" he sneered. It was not a question, but a fact that he seemed to take for granted.

"Yes," said Kara abruptly. "As a matter of fact I was. Disappointed, hurt, and angry that someone I had considered a friend''—*and more*, she thought to herself—''could so easily lie to me.''

''I never said that I lived there.''

''No, but in my confused state, you let me assume so, and that is just as bad. I think that I understand why you did it, though.'' *But I need to hear it from your lips*, she pleaded silently. Michel refused to look at her, but made a pretense of stirring his coffee slowly with a spoon.

In the weeks after her return from Cologne, she had wanted to confront him, but had held back from fear of rejection. This morning, when she had learned the truth from Louis, that Michel's poverty was not only a cross to bear but also, an embarrassment to the proud artist, Kara was certain that she could convince Michel to put aside his pride for her sake. Now, faced with his obvious resentment, she wasn't so sure. Had both she and Louis been wrong? What if Michel really didn't care about her?

Kara tugged at her bottom lip with her teeth. She knew that it was an unattractive habit, but Michel still refused to look at her anyway. She took the opportunity to study him. His normally neat hair was a mass of dark curls. He sat slightly slumped as if he were exhausted, but his shoulders were tensed. She realised that he was bracing himself for a berating.

Kara forged ahead.

''I understand why you constantly pushed me away,'' she repeated, hoping that she was not wrong. ''You're embarrassed by this.'' She waved a hand to show that she meant, not the studio, but the shabby furniture and the rundown building. "And you thought that I would be embarrassed by it, too."

Michel said nothing, but inclined his head slightly to look at her. Kara's pulse quickened.

"Well, I'm not embarrassed," she said. "You panicked when I asked to see your studio, and I thought you were insulted by my audacity." Anger now agitated her voice. "And again, you let me assume that it was so. I'm not one of your spoiled childhood friends, Michel. I grew up poor. I put myself through college and then struggled for many years with a fledgling company. Poverty does not impress me one way or another, but you wouldn't know that because you never took the chance to find out." These last words fairly exploded from her, and then she wilted into the sofa. She had known that a sympathetic approach would have embarrassed Michel even more, but she had not meant to be so angry. She wondered if she had overdone it.

Michel still glared at her.

"Aren't you going to say anything?" she asked quietly. Michel shook his head. Kara fought back the tears that threatened to choke her and rose from the couch. There was nothing left for her to say. Either she had been terribly wrong or he was too proud to admit that she was right. She would probably never know which it was, but by the way his shoulders slumped in defeat, she suspected the latter. Her heart went out to him and, in that moment, she knew that she truly loved him. Every man she met in the future would be compared to him, and found lacking. She also knew a hurt like none before: The man she loved valued his pride more than her devotion.

Her eyes blurred with tears. She stumbled toward the door, banging into Michel and knocking his cup to the floor, splashing her jeans with tepid coffee. He grabbed her shoulders to steady her, and suddenly they were face to face. Scant inches of sunlight separated them.

She looked into his eyes. Even the crazy long eyelashes couldn't mask the bitterness she saw there.

Suddenly, he crushed her to him. His lips claimed hers in a kiss. His hands gripped her shoulders as if to break her in two. He seemed to want to devour her, and then, he pushed her away.

"Is that what you want?" he asked hoarsely. "For us to fall in love, only to be forever separated by our different worlds?" His words were harsh, but the glare had left his eyes and he searched her face eagerly, looking for encouragement.

"I'm already in love with you," she said softly.

He groaned and pulled her toward him, this time into an embrace. She laid her head on his chest, feeling like she had finally come home.

"Oh, Kara. I'm so sorry. I didn't want this to happen. All my life I have searched for a woman who could appreciate my sense of fun as well as my ambition, and well . . . I finally found you." He touched her gently under the chin and tilted her head up to meet his gaze. "But my life is a mess, Kara. I work all hours. When I'm not working, I'm traveling to promote shows. I never know where my next dollar will come from. How could I ask you to live with that? And how could I ask you to wait until things are different? I'm sorry that I wasn't strong enough to say these things to your face. I just couldn't . . ."

Kara didn't want him to finish his sentence. She couldn't bear that lost-little-boy look in his eyes.

"I respect your need to prove yourself," she said, "but in Cologne you told me that I shouldn't feel responsible for other people's lives. Well, right back at you, Michel. I'm a grown woman. I can take care of myself."

Michel sank down into the chair and ran his fingers through his hair, as if to clear his mind.

"Do you know the number-one reason why couples divorce?" he asked. Kara shook her head. "Money. You deserve better than that, Kara. And I hoped that one day I could give you better." She looked at him, her expression confused. He pulled her down onto the chair with him. They were cramped into the small space. Their thighs pressed together. Michel put his arm around her shoulder to make more room. He touched her hair lightly. Kara closed her eyes and could almost imagine that they were back in Germany.

"I never stopped thinking about you." His voice was warm in her ear. "Look." She opened her eyes. He pointed at a series of three paintings that rested against the far wall. One was a dark tower like the Dom. The bell flashed in the moonlight and right beside it was a lone figure like the paintings at the

Westmount Gallery, but when Kara looked closely, she realized that it was not one figure but two, clutched together in such a tight embrace that they seemed but one. The other two paintings were similar. One was the sketch that he had done at the old port, but instead of standing alone, the girl was being embraced from behind by a mysterious man. The last one was a gazebo, with a river flowing by. Fireflies—or perhaps fairies—lit the night around it. Leaning against the gazebo railing was, again, the two figures made one by an embrace.

"I realize that I was callous not to call you," said Michel, after several seconds. He paused, perhaps hoping that Kara would deny this. When she didn't he went on.

"It was not really callousness, though, but weakness. I couldn't stand to watch you be hurt. I knew that it would break my resolve. I was sure that my success, financial success, as an artist was not long off—I still am sure—and I thought that if I could stand on my own two feet, then we could be together.

"I love you too, Kara S. Mackenzie. I have never felt so close to someone, but I couldn't in all fairness ask you to wait for me. I even hoped that you would see the article in the paper and despise me, to ease your hurt and"—he grinned a little sheepishly—"to keep you away until I could make my fortune, as they say."

With a pang of guilt, Kara realized that she almost did stay away.

"And what did you plan to do after that to win back my affection?" she asked.

"I hadn't really thought that far," admitted Michel, "I just knew that I couldn't ask you to wait. I guess I hoped that when I was ready you would still be there, but I felt like screaming every time I imagined you out on a date with another man." Kara was startled by his vehemence. "I couldn't sleep," he continued. "At night I would lay awake thinking of you, so I painted. These past months have been my most productive ever. I have enough canvases for three new shows."

"You stubborn old goat," said Kara, pushing away from him slightly, so that she could look at him. "You have no right to ask me to wait." Michel nodded, accepting her sentence, expecting her to despise him for his cowardice. "And I won't wait any longer," she continued. "As far as I'm concerned, Mr. Vernier, you already are a success. I mean, look at this work!" She pointed to the jumble of canvases around the room. "Success is not measured in dollars. You're an artist. You can't put a price on the emotions your paintings evoke. Even if you could . . ." She struggled with her thoughts. How could she make him understand that none of that mattered? She thought of the panic she had felt when she was faced with downsizing her company and had an inspiration.

"If In-A-Wink went bankrupt tomorrow would you think any less of me?"

"Of course not," he blurted, and then stopped as

if he had been caught in the act of stealing cookies, but a light of comprehension went on in his head. None of it mattered, and he couldn't let her walk away again.

"Oh, Kara, I love you. To think of all those times I pushed you away!" He pulled her onto his lap and nuzzled his face into her neck. "Can you ever forgive me?"

"Only if you lend me a pair of sweat pants. My jeans are soaked in coffee."

"Well, you always were a clumsy thing," he said, laughing, but before he got up he wrapped his arms around her so tightly that, looking on from afar, they would have seemed like one figure, not two.